THE Worst Witch
IN TROUBLE

JILL MURPHY

CANDLEWICK PRESS
CAMBRIDGE, MASSACHUSETTS

A BAD SPELL FOR THE
Worst Witch

CHAPTER ONE

IT WAS the very first day of Mildred Hubble's second year at Miss Cackle's Academy for Witches.

The school year at the academy was divided into two long terms, the first of these commencing in September and stretching right to the end of January. This was known as the Winter Term and was followed by a month of welcome holiday. The second session began in March and finished at the end of July, and this was called the Summer Term, though in fact it was still extremely cold and wintry when term began. Then there was another glorious month of holiday until the beginning of September, and the start of another year.

After her disastrous first year at the academy, it was something of a miracle that Mildred was returning there at all. She was one of those unfortunate people who seem to invite disaster wherever they go. Despite her efforts to be helpful and well behaved, Mildred had an uncanny knack of appearing to be the cause of any trouble which was occurring, and it must be admitted that there *were* occasions (particularly when her rather wild imagination ran away with her) when she managed to turn some peaceful event into a scene of total chaos.

However, *this* year Mildred was older and hopefully wiser (at any rate she was more full of good intentions than ever) and she was quite determined to lose

her reputation as the worst witch in the school.

Arriving on her broomstick at the prisonlike school gates, Mildred peered through the railings into the misty playground. For once she was early and there were only a handful of girls in the yard, all stamping their feet and huddling in their cloaks to keep out the bitter cold. It was always chilly at the school because the building was made of stone, rather like a castle, and was perched on the topmost peak of a mountain, surrounded by

3

pine trees which grew so close together that it was very damp and gloomy. In fact, the girls suffered permanently from colds and flu from all the time they were forced to spend in the freezing playground.

"Healthy fresh air!" Miss Drill, the gym mistress, would bark, herding the sneezing, coughing pupils outside. "It'll do you all a power of good. Five hundred lines to anyone caught sneaking in before the bell!"

Mildred flew over the gates and landed expertly on the other side.

"Well, *that's* a good start!" she thought, looking around in the hope that someone had witnessed so successful a landing, but of course they hadn't. People were only ever watching when she did something dreadful, never at a moment of triumph.

Mildred took her suitcase from the back of the broomstick which was hovering politely, waiting for the next command. Then she turned her attention to the tabby cat still spread-eagled on the back of the broom with its eyes screwed tightly shut and its claws gripping on for dear life. The poor little cat had never got over its terror of flying, and Mildred always had to prise it from the broomstick whenever she arrived anywhere.

"Trust *me* to get a cat like you," said Mildred fondly, stroking it with one hand and unclasping its claws with the other. "Come on, silly, we're here. Look! It's all over, you can jump off now."

The cat opened one eye cautiously, saw that it was true, and sprang onto Mildred's shoulder, where it rubbed its head gratefully against her hair. Mildred felt a wave of tenderness towards the scrawny creature.

"Mildred! Millie! It's *me!*" shrieked a familiar voice from above. Mildred looked up and saw Maud swooping over the gates, waving her hat in the air. This last action nearly caused her to fall off and she lurched to a rather drunken halt at Mildred's feet.

"Oh, Maud!" laughed Mildred, full of joy at the sight of her best friend after the long summer holiday. "Gosh, you look a lot thinner, and your hair's got longer."

"I know," said Maud, stroking her hair,

which was in two stubby plaits instead of her usual bunches. "Mother put me on this *awful* diet. I wasn't allowed to eat *anything* except lettuce and celery and dreadful stuff like that. Still, I'm out of her clutches now, so it's back to good old school dinners. Three cheers for date-pudding and custard, I say!" They both laughed.

"I don't know why they bother to *have* gates at this school," remarked Mildred, as another three pupils soared over the wall on their brooms.

"Perhaps it's in case we have some

ordinary visitors," said Maud. "You know, people who don't have brooms. Miss Cackle couldn't expect ordinary guests to bring ladders with them, could she? Who else has arrived, by the way? Anyone *we* know?"

"Only Ethel," replied Mildred. "She pretended not to see me though, not that I *care*, of course."

Ethel Hallow was the form sneak and goody-goody, and it was hardly surprising that Mildred felt unfriendly towards her after all the mean tricks Ethel had played during their first two terms, including almost getting Mildred expelled on two occasions.

"Oh, look, Maud!" said Mildred, indicating two small girls in brand-new hats and huge cloaks which nearly touched their brand-new shining boots. "They must be first-years; look at them. Don't they look *little*?"

"To think *we* were like that," said Maud in a motherly way. "It makes me feel quite old."

The two first-years were standing close together, looking lost and shy. One of them was glancing nervously around, and the other was trying unsuccessfully to stop crying. They were a sorry-looking pair. Both were thin; the weeping one had a pinched, pale face and wispy mouse-coloured hair, and the other one had brilliant orange frizzy bunches. For some reason, the weeping one reminded Mildred very strongly of someone else, though she couldn't think who it was.

"Let's go and cheer them up, shall we?" suggested Mildred. "They can't help being new, poor things. Remember how awful *we* felt?"

Feeling very grown-up and wise, Maud and Mildred sauntered casually over to the two pathetic little girls.

"Hello," said Mildred. "You must be new."

"Yes," chorused the girls.

Mildred patted the snivelling one awkwardly on the shoulder. "Don't cry," she said stiffly. "It isn't *that* bad, you know." Unfortunately, Mildred's kindly gesture only served to make matters worse, instead of better, for the girl burst into deafening sobs and flung her arms round Mildred's waist.

Mildred was appalled. Everyone in the playground was staring at her, and any minute now Miss Hardbroom (Mildred's

terrifying form mistress from the previous year) was bound to appear and accuse her of upsetting a poor new girl.

Maud detached the girl rather roughly and gave her a shake. "Stop that silly noise at once!" she said crossly. "You'll get Mildred into trouble before the first bell's even rung."

Mildred smoothed her cloak. "What's your name?" she asked.

"Sybil," snuffled the girl.

"Mine's Clarice," volunteered the other one.

"Are the teachers strict here?" asked Sybil, wiping her eyes with a corner of her voluminous cloak.

"Not really," replied Maud.

"Well, Miss Hardbroom is," said Mildred. "In fact she's the worst of the lot, and she'll be *your* form mistress. We're lucky this year because we'll get Miss Gimlett, and she's quite nice. But Miss *Hardbroom's*

horrendous. She just *appears* out of thin air—" At this point Mildred broke off and looked around in case she had done just that, but she hadn't.

"—*And* she says dreadful things to you in front of the whole class and makes you feel really stupid," continued Maud.

"That's right," said Mildred, "and *I* heard tell that she changed *one* girl into a frog because she was two seconds late for a lesson. I don't know if it's true, but there *is* a frog sometimes seen near the pond in the backyard, and I've heard that it's *really* a poor first-year who—"

"I've never heard that before!" gasped Maud. "*Is* it true?"

"I *think* so," answered Mildred, though in fact she had made up the tale on the spur of the moment and it had somehow got rather out of hand. To be honest, Mildred's stories often got rather out of hand, when she would find, to her dismay, that the whole class was listening and believing every word. She just *couldn't* say then that she'd made it all up.

Poor Sybil believed every word of Mildred's story about the frog and she burst into renewed and even noisier sobs, so deafening that Maud and Mildred thought it best to scurry away, leaving Clarice to offer comfort.

"Mildred! Maudie! Yoo-hoo! It's *me*!"

Enid Nightshade, the new girl who arrived last term and was now their friend, came zooming over the treetops and screeched to a halt so forcefully that her

cat and suitcase shot off the back, and Maud and Mildred had to leap out of the way to avoid being run over.

At that moment the bell rang and the three witches picked up all their belongings and struggled inside with them.

"Thank goodness we haven't got H.B. anymore," whispered Enid. (H.B. was their nickname for Miss Hardbroom.)

"Yes," agreed Mildred. "This year should be as easy as pie without *her* breathing down our necks."

CHAPTER TWO

THE FIRST announcement made by Miss Cackle at assembly was the ghastly news that Miss Hardbroom had changed places with Miss Gimlett, and would now be accompanying her old form into their second year. An audible groan rippled through the new Form Two, quelled at once by one of Miss Hardbroom's piercing glances, which always made each pupil feel that they had been noticed personally.

With a sinking heart, Mildred moved miserably through all the chores of the first day, unpacking robes, arranging the new books in her desk, feeding the cat, and innumerable small tasks till at last it was bedtime.

The pupils were too depressed to bother sneaking into each other's rooms for a chat as they usually did on the first night back at school. Mildred lay in a glum heap under the blankets with the cat purring like a lawn mower on her pillow, trying to think if there was any possible advantage in another year with Miss Hardbroom at the helm, but there wasn't.

Next morning, Mildred was jolted awake by the bell ringing in a much more frantic way than usual. It didn't take long for the cobwebs of sleep to clear and for her to realize that it was the fire bell.

An untidily dressed Maud flung open Mildred's door as she rushed past. "Quick, Mil!" she shrieked. "It's fire drill, come on!"

"What a time to choose," said Mildred,

bundling on her tunic over her pyjamas. "Perhaps it's a real fire?"

Maud went rushing off down the corridor, but Mildred stopped and looked out of the window to see if there was any evidence of fire. There, in the yard below, was Miss Hardbroom wreathed in thick purple smoke. She appeared to be standing in her customary arms-folded, upright posture, staring into the smoke as if she was in a trance, which seemed decidedly odd, given the circumstances.

"Crumbs!" thought Mildred. "She's gone into a state of shock. I'll have to help!"

Mildred rushed to the washroom and seized the bucket which stood under the window there to catch drips from the leak in the ceiling. It was already half full with stagnant rainwater, so Mildred filled it to the brim, then carried it back to the yard windowsill, collecting her broomstick on the way.

She peered out of the window again, hoping that she might perhaps have imagined the scene below, but Miss Hardbroom had not moved and was now almost hidden from view by the smoke.

"Here goes!" said Mildred, her spirits rising as she thought how grateful her form mistress would be. "Perhaps I'll get a medal for bravery."

It is difficult, at the best of times, to balance on a broomstick, but when you are trying to carry a heavy bucket of water at the same time, it is virtually impossible. Mildred did her best to arrange the bucket hanging from the back, but it was obviously going to spill the minute they took off, so she put the bucket back onto the windowsill, climbed onto the broom first, and then settled the bucket in her lap. This

seemed to be reasonably steady, so taking
her courage in both hands, Mildred gave
the word: "Down, broom! Fast!"

Instantly they plunged into a vertical
nosedive so abrupt that the bucket flew
from her grasp and dropped like a stone.
Mildred swooped desperately after it but,
alas, too late. A torrent of foul, icy water

drenched Miss Hardbroom from head to toe, followed a second later by the bucket, which crashed over her head with a doom-laden clang. To give the stern form mistress some credit, it must be recorded that she did not flinch when the metal bucket struck after falling from such a height.

Though her natural inclination was to turn round and zoom straight back again, Mildred could see that there was no escape. The smoke had cleared, revealing at least half the school lined up in rows and Miss Hardbroom still in the same position, with the bucket neatly over her head. For a mad moment, Mildred thought that perhaps, for some unknown reason, it was only a statue of Miss Hardbroom, but this illusion was shattered when the statue spoke.

"There is no need to ask *which* pupil is responsible for this," came the familiar voice from inside the bucket. "Mildred Hubble, perhaps you would be kind enough to assist me in my predicament?"

The sight of any other teacher dripping with water and with a bucket over her head would have been an occasion for great mirth among the pupils, but absolutely nothing could diminish Miss Hardbroom's

power. Not a sound was heard, not a smirk flickered on any face as Mildred stepped forward and stood on tiptoe to remove the bucket.

Miss Hardbroom's eyes bored into Mildred like a laser beam the moment they came into view.

"Thank you, Mildred," she said acidly.

"I—I'm s-sorry, M-M-Miss Hardb-bb-room," gibbered Mildred. "It was—I thought you were on fire—there was smoke so I, well I thought—it seemed . . ."

"Mildred," said Miss Hardbroom heavily, "does it seem likely to you that I would be standing here in the middle of a raging inferno, casually rounding up all you girls?"

"There was the smoke, Miss Hardbroom," explained Mildred in a tiny voice, suddenly feeling aware of the striped pyjama legs under her tunic.

"*If* you remember your fire drill Mildred," said Miss Hardbroom, "pupils are expected in the yard through the main door, and *not,* as some girls seem to imagine, from the upstairs windows. On entering the yard through the *correct* entrance, they would have been met by me, who would then have informed them that the smoke was merely magic smoke to lend atmosphere to the proceedings and that there

was no cause for total panic as some pupils would seem to be prone to."

"Yes, Miss Hardbroom," quavered Mildred. "I'm sorry, Miss Hardbroom."

"Get into line, Mildred," ordered Miss Hardbroom. "Let us just say that we expect this to be your only half-witted jape for the entire term. Ethel? Would you please fetch me a towel and my cloak before I turn into an iceberg?"

"Of course, Miss Hardbroom," said Ethel, smiling demurely at her form mistress, but pulling a horrid face at Mildred as she passed her by.

Mildred lined up next to her two friends, Maud and Enid.

"You are the limit, Mildred," whispered Maud.

"I *know*," said Mildred miserably. "I must have been still asleep or something."

"Actually," said Enid, "it was quite funny really."

At this point all three friends felt an unruly wave of amusement sweeping over them, and the rest of the fire drill was spent desperately avoiding each other's eyes in case a fit of the giggles should descend, and they were all agreed (especially Mildred) that this would definitely *not* be the thing to do.

CHAPTER THREE

FIRE DRILL was followed immediately by breakfast in the dining hall and everyone was surprised to see Ethel deliberately sitting down next to Mildred, for it was common knowledge that the two were not on the best of terms. "You haven't changed, I see," remarked Ethel provokingly.

Mildred ignored this jibe and sprinkled sugar over her bowl of porridge which resembled a drought-stricken riverbed.

"Actually," continued Ethel, "I've got a bone to pick with you, Mildred Hubble."

"Oh?" said Mildred. "What?"

"It's about terrorizing my little sister," replied Ethel.

"I don't even *know* your little sister!" exclaimed Mildred.

"Really?" said Ethel. "Are you sure you don't remember telling a poor little girl named Sybil some stupid story about being turned into a frog?"

"Gosh, was that your sister?" asked Mildred.

"Yes, it *was,* as a matter of fact," replied Ethel.

"I don't know why we didn't notice, Mil," said Maud, rallying to her friend's side. "We should have noticed that spiky nose anywhere."

Ethel turned deep mauve with rage.

"Oh, come *on,* Ethel," said Mildred, trying to make peace. "It *was* only a made-up story. She *was* being a bit of a weed, and in any case I went to cheer her up in the first place."

"A fine way to cheer people up!" retorted Ethel. "Terrifying the wits out of them. Sybil still hasn't got over the shock, and don't you go insulting my family. Sybil's delicate, not a weed."

"*Look*, Ethel," said Mildred firmly, "just stop it, will you? I'm not getting into a fight over some silly little first-year whether she's your sister or not, and if you'll excuse me, this porridge is bad enough hot, but cold it's inedible and there's a long way to go till lunchtime."

"I won't forget this," muttered Ethel. "No one insults *my* family and gets away with it."

"Weed!" exclaimed Mildred, feeling suddenly reckless after all Ethel's prodding. "All you Hallows are weeds, weeds, weeds!"

Ethel got up and flounced out of the hall, looking grim.

"You shouldn't goad her," said Enid. "You know what she's like."

"I know," said Mildred, "but she does ask for it sometimes with all her airs and graces. No one insults *my* family," she mimicked in Ethel's voice. "She's just an old windbag. She'll have forgotten by tomorrow."

"I wouldn't be too sure about *that*," warned Maud.

35

After breakfast, Miss Hardbroom announced that the rest of the morning would be devoted to cat training. All the girls were presented with black kittens in their first term at the academy and these were trained to ride on the back of their broomsticks. Mildred, however, had been given a rather dim-witted tabby because there hadn't been quite enough black ones to go round. It seemed rather typical of her luck that she had ended up with the wrong sort of cat, and she couldn't help wondering if Miss Hardbroom had made sure that the misfit kitten had been given to Mildred, rather than to someone like Ethel.

"I hope you have all been practising during the holiday," said Miss Hardbroom, as the girls all lined up with their brooms hovering next to them and the cats perched on the back—that is to say, *most* of the cats were perched on the back. Mildred's tabby

was clinging desperately to the front of her cardigan, its claws hooked in and a wild, desperate look on its face.

"The cat is supposed to be on the broomstick, Mildred," said Miss Hardbroom wearily.

"Yes, Miss Hardbroom," agreed Mildred, dragging the cat from her front and reducing the cardigan to shreds at the same time. The desperate creature immediately spread itself flat on the back of the broom with its eyes glued shut as if awaiting execution.

"How many terms have you been training that cat, Mildred?" said Miss Hardbroom. "Look at the other cats. None of *them* seem to be finding it so terribly difficult to just *sit* on their brooms. It is not as though they were being asked to do an aerobatic display, Mildred. Now take that cat to your room and work with it there for the rest of the morning. The creature is not fit to be seen until it is properly trained. It is a disgrace to the academy."

"Yes, Miss Hardbroom," said Mildred, now faced with the embarrassing task of prising the unfortunate cat from the broomstick and making her way miserably from the yard with the taunting stare of Ethel boring into her back.

Inside her room, Mildred decided to get into bed for a few minutes to warm up. It was a freezing cold day and her feet were like blocks of ice after the session in the yard. The cat, delighted that its ordeal was over, burrowed under the covers like a furry hot-water bottle, and although Mildred had only meant to sit and get warm, within a few minutes her eyelids began to droop, and before long she was fast asleep — *so* fast asleep that she did not hear the door opening very quietly.

CHAPTER FOUR

THE NOISE of the bedroom door being slammed woke Mildred with a start. She opened her eyes and froze with horror and disbelief at the sight of a vast creature staring down at her with green eyes each as big as a lily pond.

Mildred closed her eyes again, hoping that perhaps it was only a nightmare, but when she sneaked another look, the apparition was still there, and now it began patting gently at Mildred with its gigantic paws.

Terrified, Mildred backed away and crashed into something hard, which seemed to be a huge iron railing towering above her. However, at this distance from the monster, she could see that it was none other than her own tabby cat, which for some reason had grown to the size of a mammoth.

Knowing the cat as well as she did, Mildred could see that, despite its size, it was frightened out of its wits. Her suspicions flew at once to Ethel having cast a spell on the cat to get even with Mildred for the insult to Ethel's family.

"Don't be scared, Tab," she started to say, but much to her surprise, all that came out was a strange hoarse noise sounding rather like "Craark!"

Panic began to grip Mildred as it slowly dawned on her that not only Tabby, but also the bedstead, all the furniture, and even the bats sleeping round the picture

rail were many times larger than usual. This led her to the alarming conclusion that it was not *they* who were bigger, but *she* who was smaller—and a *lot* smaller.

She peered over the edge of the bed-stead and saw a cliff of bedcover stretching endlessly to the stone floor. Tabby began purring, which sounded, to the miniature Mildred, like a squadron of aeroplanes taking off.

"Oh, do stop it, Tab. I can't hear myself think!" she tried to say, but once again the words seemed to stick in her throat and come out as a croak.

Mildred decided to get to the chest of drawers, on which stood a small mirror, so that she could see just how small she was. The end of the bedstead was only a few inches away from the drawers, but in her new tiny condition it appeared to be miles. However, to her great surprise, she suddenly felt the impulse to take a flying leap at the huge gap, and landed with the ease of an acrobat on top of the chest.

"How strange," thought Mildred. "I had no idea that I could jump like that!"

She soon discovered why, and it was not a pleasant discovery. Looking back at her from the mirror, with eyes like saucers, was a small, olive-green frog. Mildred turned round, but there was no one behind her. She stretched out her hand and saw a green, damp limb reach out to touch the mirror frog's webbed foot. Mildred

began to cry, and as she lifted her hand to wipe away the tears she watched with horrified fascination as the reflection did the same.

"This is no use at all," Mildred said to herself sternly. "Sitting here crying isn't going to change anything. I must get help."

She jumped back onto the bed and noticed something lying on the pillow. It was a giant-sized clump of weeds—Ethel's way of telling Mildred who had cast the spell and why.

Mildred leapt to the floor and sat there for a moment, reflecting on how nice it was to be able to jump such an amazing distance without getting hurt. It reminded her of the disastrous pole vault on the school sports day, when Enid had cast a spell on Mildred's pole to help her, but had inadvertently overdone the magic and Mildred had sailed through Miss Hardbroom's study window.

However, the ability to jump was the *only* pleasant aspect of Mildred's new condition, and a sudden, hot wave of panic seized her. She felt utterly trapped in her small, cramped frog's body, her knees felt bent in the wrong place and her arms were too short, and it was quite terrifying trying to speak and only being capable of a hoarse croaking sound. There was a large gap beneath Mildred's door, and she decided to set off and find someone to help her. Watched by her baffled cat,

Mildred squeezed through the gap and hopped away down the corridor, convinced that *nothing* could be worse than just sitting helplessly in her room.

As it turned out, she would have done better to have stayed on her pillow, for there she might have been found by Maud or Enid, who would possibly have put two and two together at the curious sight of a cat and frog nestling on the same bed. But outside her room, Mildred was just a common frog who had strayed into the school, where it would be unlikely to occur to anyone (except the wicked person who had done the deed) that it might be a second-year witch under an enchantment.

CHAPTER FIVE

WITH THE worst possible timing, Mildred turned the corner just as Miss Hardbroom strode through the door leading from the yard.

"Well, well," she said, bending down and picking up the little frog, "what have we here, then?" And without further ado, she crammed Mildred into her pocket and marched off.

It was not very pleasant in the pocket. Mildred felt around in the bumping, musty darkness and discovered a whistle, a notebook with a rubber band round it, and a voluminous handkerchief.

The next thing she knew, Miss Hardbroom had pulled her out of the pocket and plonked her unceremoniously into a high-sided glass jar. Through the glass she saw that she was on a shelf in the potion laboratory and the tall figure of her form mistress was swirling out of the door.

Mildred felt absolutely dreadful. There appeared to be no way of escaping and even if she *did* escape, she had no idea what to do. She wondered if Ethel would relent and change her back, or whether she might be really wicked enough to leave her as a frog forever. She also wondered if Miss Hardbroom and the class would begin to wonder where she was after a while.

They were wondering where she was at that very moment. Miss Hardbroom had, in fact, been on her way to Mildred's room when she encountered the frog. After leaving the potion laboratory, she soon discovered that Mildred was not in her room and set off to look all over the school, where, of course, she did not find the missing pupil. The class, when questioned, did not know where Mildred was either. It was a mystery.

"Perhaps she's run away?" suggested Enid to Maud as the girls trooped in for dinner. "H.B. was cross with her about the cat."

"I don't think so," said Maud. "She would have taken the cat with her if she'd done that."

"Well, I can't think *where* she is then," shrugged Enid.

"Nor can I," said Maud. "But if you ask *me*, Ethel's got something to do with it. She's got that *look* on. You know, that *I*-know-something-*you*-don't sort of look."

"We'd better keep an eye on her then," said Enid.

Meanwhile, in the potion laboratory, Mildred was desperately trying to over-balance the jar by climbing up the side

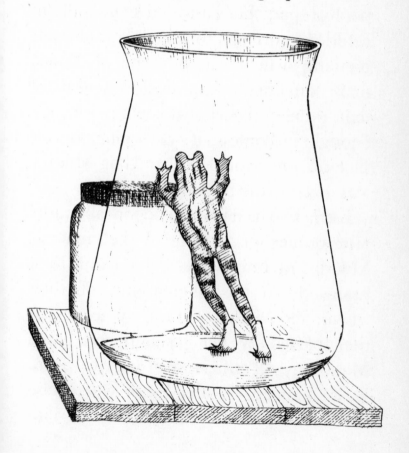

and leaning on it. However, she could only get up a little way before she tumbled backwards, as the jar had a heavy glass base which proved impossible to overbalance. After several tries, she gave up and wept a pool of panicky, frustrated tears. All she could do now was to rely on Ethel being merciful (which was not one of Ethel's main qualities). Also, Mildred realized that even if Ethel *was* feeling merciful enough to confess, it was quite possible that no one would realize that Mildred was actually the frog in the jar.

Form Two filed into the potion laboratory after dinner for an hour of spell making. Maud and Enid were still racking their brains as to the whereabouts of their friend, and Mildred felt utterly helpless as they passed by her jar and she heard Maud say, "Perhaps she *has* run away, Enid. I mean, I can't think where else she's gone, and she knows she'll get into the most dreadful trouble if she turns up now without a good excuse."

"I'm *here!*" Mildred tried to shriek, but it only came out as a frenzied croaking.

"That is the noisiest frog I've ever had in this laboratory," snapped Miss Hardbroom with a piercing glance at the jar. Mildred lapsed into silence and fixed her eyes on Maud in the hope that she might be able to send some sort of message through the air like a radio wave to her friend. It almost succeeded.

"Enid," said Maud, as they sorted through the ingredients for an invisibility potion, "I'm sure that frog's staring at me.

It hasn't taken its eyes off our table for the last ten minutes."

"Don't be silly," said Enid, "Frogs don't stare at people."

"Well, that one does," said Maud. "Look!" Enid looked. The little frog was definitely gazing hard in Maud's direction, and when it saw Enid turn to look, it began jumping up and down and croaking like a mad thing.

"Maud," said Miss Hardbroom, "would you please remove that frog from the jar and put it into the box in the cupboard? We do not wish to listen to that noise all afternoon."

"CRAARK!" pleaded Mildred. "CRAARK! CRAAARK! CRAAAARK!" Maud approached the shelf cautiously, reached into the jar, and took Mildred out.

Mildred gave one last, long look into Maud's eyes, but she could see that there was no hope of Maud recognizing a half-

mad frog as her best friend. There was nothing for it but to flee.

Mildred leapt into the air as high as her new, powerful legs would take her, and landed with a soft "splat" on Maud and Enid's bench.

"Don't just *stand* there girls!" bellowed Miss Hardbroom, "Catch the creature!"

The entire class took off in pursuit of the frog as it sprang nimbly from bench to bench. Hands clutched and faces loomed, and suddenly Mildred remembered that the class would be making an invisibility potion. (Miss Hardbroom had told them to study for it after breakfast.) Mildred dived for Ethel's bench, knowing that Ethel would have made the best potion of all, and there it was, dark green and bubbling in the cauldron, with a half-full test tube conveniently spilling a puddle of the liquid onto the bench. Mildred's frog tongue shot out and lapped as much as it could.

"Oh, Miss Hardbroom!" she heard Ethel cry. "The frog's disappeared!"

Mildred heaved a sigh of relief and leapt onto the floor, where she huddled in perfect silence under the bookcase near the door.

"How very strange," mused Miss Hardbroom. "Not only the noisiest, but also the most knowledgeable frog I have ever been privileged to meet."

"I'm sure it was trying to tell me something," whispered Maud to Enid. "Perhaps it knows something about Mildred?"

"What could a *frog* know?" asked Enid.

Maud shrugged her shoulders. "*I* don't know," she replied, "but it was no ordinary frog. I can tell you *that* for certain."

CHAPTER SIX

COWERING beneath the bookcase, Mildred dared not move in case she had begun to be visible again. (When you have taken an invisibility potion, you reappear very gradually, head first, followed by the rest of the body.)

In fact, being invisible is a very odd sensation indeed. Imagine holding out your leg and feeling it with your invisible hand while being unable actually to see it. For this reason, walking becomes rather a difficult experience, as you can feel your feet moving along but cannot see where they are going. This means that you often find yourself moving in the opposite direction to the one intended, which, of course, is extremely annoying.

Mildred held out her arm to see if it had begun to reappear, but it hadn't. Her patience paid off at last when she heard Miss Hardbroom tell the girls to pack up their books, and after much clattering and bustling, the door closed and the laboratory fell silent.

Mildred hopped out and looked around. As usual, there was a gap of several inches under the door. In fact, it seemed to be a school speciality that none of the doors fitted properly and the windows (most of which were slit windows) had no glass in them at all. The whole school seemed to have been designed with the sole purpose of freezing all the pupils to death.

Mildred squeezed through the gap and

set off as fast as possible along the corridor and down the spiral staircase to the yard. From there she hopped to the pond at the back of the school, for she felt sure that she could hide safely there in the weeds and rushes while she tried to find some solution to her appalling problem.

Sitting on a stone in the middle of the water was the large frog that Mildred had often seen, and which had been the inspiration for the tale which had scared Ethel's sister.

"Craark!" it said, and to Mildred's delight, she found that she could understand what the creature meant. It said, "What on earth's the matter with you? Where's the rest of your body?"

Mildred realized that her head had reappeared, which must have looked rather alarming, bobbing about all over the place with no body attached.

"Don't be afraid," said Mildred. "I've taken an invisibility potion and I'm just coming back into view. You'll be able to see all of me in a moment."

"Where did you get the potion from?" asked the frog, slipping silently from the stone and swimming across to Mildred's head.

"Oh, dear," said Mildred, "it's a long story. I'm not really a frog at all. I'm a second-year witch at the school, and this beastly girl called Ethel Hallow has changed me into a frog, and I was—"

"Good gracious me!" exclaimed the frog. "This is quite amazing! *I'm* not a frog either. I'm a magician. What a wonderful coincidence. I've been here for years, and this is the first conversation I've had with a human for simply ages. How extraordinary! Well, well, well, I can scarcely believe it. Allow me to offer you a nice fly from my store."

"A *fly*?" repeated Mildred.

"Oh, dear," said the frog magician. "Of course, you've only been a frog for a while. A fly, my dear—you know, bzzzzzz. They really are quite delicious once you get used to the idea. I nearly starved at first because I couldn't bear the idea of eating—well— insects and the like, but it's amazing what you can get used to."

Mildred grimaced. "I'm hoping to be changed back before I get used to it," she said (with considerable spirit, bearing in mind how hopeless she felt). "Tell me how you got here in the first place."

"Well, my dear," said the frog magician, settling fatly onto a stone. "It was so long ago that I've almost forgotten. Let me see. . . . Yes, well in those days, of course, the castle was not a school. It was used for meetings and conferences of magicians. We used to have a lovely 'do' in the summer. Like a holiday camp it was, endless teas and lectures and displays of magic all afternoon. Anyway, to cut a long story short, I had an argument—rather like *you* did, by the sound of it—with a fellow magician, and this was the result. Before I could persuade him to change his mind, the summer was over, everyone went home, and I was left behind. I've been here ever since. I must admit I get very glum sometimes." He breathed a huge sigh and gazed into the dark water.

"Why don't you come with *me*?" said Mildred brightly. "I'm going to find my friend Maud, after dark. I know I can make her understand, and then she'll be able to help me. She'll help you, too."

A large tear splashed from the frog

magician's eye. "It's no use," he croaked sadly. "It's got to be a magician who takes off the spell. There aren't any in the school, are there?"

"No, there aren't," said Mildred thoughtfully. "All right, then, I'll go to find Maud by myself, but I'll come back for you as soon as I'm changed back, and I'll get you to a magician somehow. I won't forget."

"You're very kind, my dear—what is your name?" said the frog magician.

"Mildred Hubble," replied Mildred. "What's yours?"

"Algernon—er—something-or-other Webb. Isn't that awful?" said the frog magician. "Do you know I can't remember the first bit, I've been here so long? What was it now? Bowen-Webb? Stone-Webb? Or was it Webbley-Stone? I'm sorry, child, I've completely forgotten. Oh, dear, it was all so very long ago. I must say, sometimes I'd give *anything* to have a

68

proper old-fashioned tea again, one gets so fed up with flies and water boatmen. Every now and then I can see it all so clearly; a nice log fire and a little round table with a tablecloth, and hot toast with great slabs of butter, and crumpets with honey all oozing out of the little holes, and a china cup with steaming tea—"

The memory was too much for him and he erupted into loud, desperate sobs, a pitiful sound to hear.

Mildred hopped next to him and patted him with a half-visible arm. "Don't cry, Mr. Algernon, sir," she said comfortingly. "You *shall* have crumpets for tea again; don't you worry. It'll be all right; I promise it will."

CHAPTER SEVEN

NIGHT had fallen and the pupils of the academy were all in bed. That is to say, most of the pupils were in bed. Enid had sneaked into Maud's room for a quick conference about Mildred. It was bitterly cold in the cell-like bedroom, and the two girls were huddled on the bed, wrapped in blankets, with cats draped over their feet to keep out the cold. (Maud was taking care of Mildred's tabby.)

"Well, I give up," said Enid. "If she has run away, she's left every single piece of clothing behind, even her cardigan, so she must be frozen solid by now."

"She hasn't run away," said Maud. "She wouldn't have gone just because H.B. told her off. Anyway, she's not likely to have run away without old Tabby here, especially as that was why H.B. was cross in the first place. It just doesn't make sense. No, I'm quite sure that Ethel knows something about it. Don't you remember what she said to Mildred? No one insults my family and gets away with it. Well I think she's done something really awful to Mildred."

"Like what?" asked Enid.

Just at that moment, the cats all leapt to their feet with their fur on end and looked in the direction of the door. The girls exchanged nervous glances, thinking that it

71

must be Miss Hardbroom come to reprimand them for being out of bed. Maud crept to the door and opened it very slowly.

Outside in the shadowy corridor was the little frog which had escaped from the potion laboratory. Maud and Enid could tell it was the same one because its feet had not yet reappeared.

Mildred hopped inside and was picked up by Maud, who took her over to Enid.

Tabby immediately began nuzzling up against the frog in a very friendly way, unlike the other two cats who kept in the background, backs arched and humming frantically.

"How strange, Enid!" said Maud. "Look at Tabby. It seems as if they've met before."

The two witches suddenly looked at each other in horror.

"Oh, *no!*" they exclaimed at the same time.

"It can't be!" gasped Maud. "Or can it?"

"I think it might be," replied Enid grimly. She took the frog from Maud and held it up near her face.

"Are you—" she began, but before she could finish, the little frog was leaping up and down, nodding its head and croaking so loudly that the girls were afraid someone would hear.

"Sssh!" whispered Enid. "Calm down, for goodness' sake. Now then, are you our very good friend, Mildred Hubble?"

There was no doubt about it, from the nodding and mad capering, that here was the answer to Mildred's sudden disappearance.

"Did Ethel do it?" asked Maud.

More nodding and croaking was the answer.

"Right!" said Maud. "Come on, Enid."

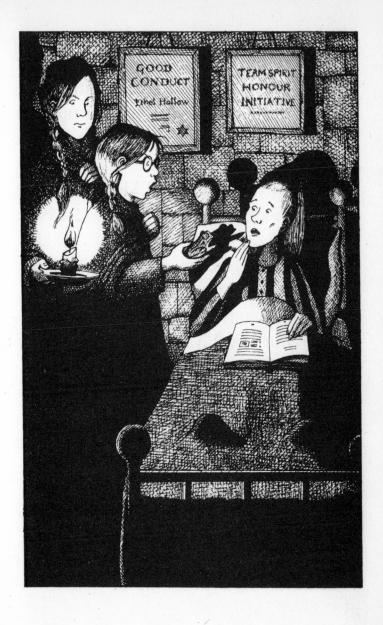

Ethel was not asleep, either. She was sitting up in bed learning the chant which was to be tested the next day. She nearly leapt through the ceiling when the door opened and Maud and Enid marched menacingly into the room.

"Recognize this?" asked Maud, holding out the frog. "Remind you of anyone, does it?"

Ethel turned white as a sheet. "I—I don't know *what* you're talking about," she said.

"All right," said Maud, "then we're off to Miss Hardbroom. Come on, Enid. Sorry to have bothered you, Ethel."

"No!" cried Ethel. "It's Mildred, isn't it? Oh, thank goodness you found her. I didn't mean her to run off and get lost. I just wanted to give her a fright, that's all. Come here and let me take off the spell."

"Hold on a moment," said Enid. "I think we'd *better* get Miss Hardbroom. I mean, how are we going to explain where Mildred's been?"

"Let's tell her in the morning, wheedled Ethel. "She'll be in a dreadful mood if we disturb her tonight. Anyway, I'm sure poor Mildred here can't wait a moment longer."

Ethel spoke the words of the spell, and at once Mildred was standing before them.

"Thanks for nothing, Ethel Hallow," she said, rubbing her arms and legs. "Gosh, it feels really odd to be this big again. Oh Maud, it was so awful in the potion lab, I really thought I'd had it."

The door opened like a thunderclap, and there stood Miss Hardbroom.

"Having a little party, are we, girls?" she inquired drily. "Ah, Mildred, I see you've decided to rejoin us at last. We hope you have had a pleasant time wherever you have been. Would it be too much, perhaps, to inquire exactly where you have been, hmm?"

The three friends looked desperately at Ethel, who stepped forward with a smirk flickering at the corners of her mouth.

"I caught Mildred creeping down the corridor with Maud and Enid here," she said innocently. "So I invited them into my room and I was just coming to fetch you, Miss Hardbroom."

"Ethel!" exclaimed Maud, Enid and Mildred together.

"That's not *true*, Miss Hardbroom," squeaked Mildred indignantly. "Ethel turned me into a frog, and that's where I've been for the last day, and it was her fault. She's only just changed me back."

"I did *not*," lied Ethel, sounding convincingly angry. "I wouldn't do such a thing, unlike some people around here," she added under her breath, referring to the time when Mildred had accidentally changed Ethel into a pig during their first term at the school.

"Mildred," said Miss Hardbroom, "you will write out five hundred times, in perfect handwriting, 'I must learn to curb my imagination and to—' good gracious, girl! What on earth has happened to your feet?"

They all looked and saw that Mildred's feet, still recovering from the invisibility potion, had not yet reappeared, even though she had changed back to her usual self.

"That *proves* it!" exclaimed Mildred joyfully. "Miss Hardbroom, I was the frog in the potion laboratory, the one you found in the corridor, and the potion I took is only just wearing off—that's why I haven't any feet at the moment. Oh, yes! And to prove it even more, I can tell you that you have a handkerchief, a whistle, and a notebook with a rubber band round it in your pocket!"

Miss Hardbroom turned to Ethel.

"Well?" she asked, in tones so terrifying that all four of her pupils shrank back against the wall.

"I—I, well—I—she *had* insulted my f-family, Miss Hardb-broom," said Ethel feebly. "And I really didn't mean her to

run off like that. I only meant to give her
a scare. I didn't mean . . ." she trailed into
silence.

"Ethel, Mildred," said Miss Hardbroom,
"you will both come to my room first thing
in the morning before breakfast. Now get
along to bed at once, all of you."

Their form mistress ushered the three friends to their separate rooms. Mildred's room was the last of all.

"Let us hope that your feet are in the correct place by the morning, Mildred," said Miss Hardbroom frostily, as Mildred hastened inside and closed the door.

CHAPTER EIGHT

SHORTLY after the rising-bell had been rung, Ethel and Mildred were waiting anxiously outside Miss Hardbroom's door. It was the first time that Ethel had been summoned to her form mistress for any reason other than praise.

"It's *your* fault, Mildred Hubble," she muttered, as they paced up and down the corridor. "If you hadn't told that stupid story to Sybil and upset her, I wouldn't have done it to you. Anyway, I really *was* going to take the spell off straightaway, but of course *you* had to go hopping off and get caught and land us in this mess."

"*You've* got a nerve, Ethel Hallow!" said Mildred. "You just can't ever admit you might be wrong, can you? It wasn't exactly fun being pursued round the potion lab and shoved into jars. It wouldn't occur to you that—"

The door opened and Miss Hardbroom beckoned them inside.

"Sit," she barked, indicating two chairs opposite her desk. They all sat down.

"It *wasn't* my fault, Miss Hardbroom!" Ethel blurted out. "Mildred Hubble told my little sister this story about first-years being changed into frogs by the teachers. She even told Sybil that the frog in the school *pond* was enchanted, and poor Sybil was in such a state that I thought some-one ought to teach Mildred a lesson."

"It wasn't exactly like that, Miss Hardbroom," said Mildred. "I'd gone up to Ethel's sister to cheer her up because she was looking so miserable. I didn't know—"

"I have heard quite enough excuses," interrupted Miss Hardbroom, "and I do not wish to hear any more. Frankly, I am not in the least bit interested in whose fault the incident was.

"The reason I have called you both here is to remind you that you are now second-year witches, and I do not expect this ridiculous feud between you two girls to continue. Do you understand?"

"Yes, Miss Hardbroom," replied Ethel and Mildred meekly.

"Ethel," continued Miss Hardbroom, "just because you happen to be an excellent scholar and one of the most helpful members of my class, I do not expect you to lie your way out of a situation when it has become awkward. Do you understand this?"

"Yes, Miss Hardbroom," said Ethel.

"Neither," said Miss Hardbroom, "do I expect you to contravene the Witches' Code, rule number seven, paragraph two, by changing your fellows into any sort of animal for whatever reason. Do you understand *that*?"

"Yes, Miss Hardbroom," said Ethel.

"Good," said Miss Hardbroom. "Then you will understand why I am giving you one hundred lines which will say, 'I must tell the truth at all times.'"

She turned her attention to Mildred. "Mildred, I would ask you to refrain from tormenting the first-years with untrue horror stories about the academy, and to make some attempt to *think*—if that is possible—before you embark upon any more madcap escapades."

"Yes, Miss Hardbroom," replied Mildred. "Oh, and Miss Hardbroom, I've just re-membered, there *is* a frog in the pond and it really *is* someone under enchantment. I *know* it sounds like another made-up story—"

"Mildred Hubble," said Miss Hardbroom wearily, "what have I just said to you? No, don't attempt to answer. I expect you've completely forgotten already, haven't you? Sometimes I feel that any attempt to communicate with you is an utter waste of time.

"Now I have said all that I wish to say to you girls except, Mildred, that you will write one hundred lines which will say, 'I must try very hard not to be quite so silly.' Now hurry along to breakfast, girls. That will be all."

Mildred was now faced with the impossible task of convincing someone that there was an elderly magician in the pond. She tried to tell Maud and Enid, but they had had enough of frog stories, particularly as Mildred had actually admitted to them, at the time, that the story she had told Sybil was not true.

It seemed quite hopeless. The only way of getting to a magician was at the celebrations on Hallowe'en night, but after the broomstick display, which Mildred had ruined the year before, she felt very worried about creating any more havoc in that direction.

Mildred spent a lot of time by the pond telling the frog magician that she hadn't forgotten him and that she would get him out if it was the last thing she did. He always kept a distance from her, but she felt sure he knew who she was. Looking at his froggy face, half-submerged in the murky water, it was hard to believe that he really was anything more than an ordinary frog, and Mildred could see why no one had recognized her when she was in the same plight.

CHAPTER NINE

A WEEK before the Hallowe'en celebration, Miss Hardbroom entered the classroom, looking grim.

"Sit, girls," she said, looking round severely at the rows of pupils. "I have here a letter from the chief magician, Mr. Hellibore, who presides over the Hallowe'en festivities each year. In this letter he specifically requests that the girls responsible for the utter fiasco which *should* have been our broomstick display last year are to be kept away from this year's display so that he can relax and enjoy the events taking place. Those two girls were Ethel Hallow and Mildred Hubble. It is true that the incident was not actually Mildred's fault, for once, because Ethel *had* cast a spell on the broomstick which Mildred was using, but in view of our little *chat* this morning, girls"—here she darted a glance at Ethel and Mildred, who wriggled uncomfortably in their seats—"I feel this is a most fitting punishment for both of you. As you retire to your beds at dusk on the eve of Hallowe'en, perhaps you might ponder upon the exciting evening you *could* have been enjoying and resolve to end this ridiculous feud at last."

Mildred was very upset at her exclusion from Hallowe'en for several reasons. One was the awful unfairness of it all, as it really hadn't been her fault that Ethel had cast a bad spell on the broomstick she had lent to Mildred, thus ruining the display.

Also it would be very hard to stay in bed and miss the evening's fun. But, worst of all, she would not be able to take her unfortunate friend to be changed back to his normal self, and this was the only night of the whole year when she would be in the presence of a magician.

There was only one thing to do. She would have to persuade someone to change places with her, and if that didn't work, she would have to kidnap someone and *force* them to swap places. Even the thought of this plan seemed dreadful to Mildred, who could see how such a course of action was fraught with danger, but there really was no alternative if she was to help the frog magician.

Maud and Enid were the obvious people to ask, but they flatly refused.

"You must be barmy, Mildred," exclaimed Maud. "H.B. would *slaughter* us if we got caught. Anyway, what's it *for*? I mean if *I* was you, I'd just put up with it and stay in bed. Enid and I will describe it all when we come back."

"Look, Maud," pleaded Mildred, "I *know* it's hard for you to believe me, but that frog in the pond really *is* a magician, and he can only be changed back by another magician. If you don't want to change places with me, then couldn't you take him yourself and ask the chief magician for help? *Please.*"

"No way!" said Maud and Enid together.

"Honestly, Mil," said Enid gently, "I know it must have been awful when you were turned into a frog, what with the narrow squeak in the potion lab and everything, but don't you think perhaps you're getting a little *obsessed* with frogs and ponds? Maud and I have seen you down there chatting away to the empty water. Perhaps a nice evening in bed might be good for you, after all."

94

Mildred stomped away feeling desperate. If Maud and Enid thought she was mad and wouldn't help her, then no one would, and the only course of action was to go ahead with the kidnapping plan. Mildred quailed at the prospect.

The morning of the celebrations dawned, and the whole day was given over to ironing best robes, practising on broomsticks, and chanting. Mildred and Ethel sat miserably at their desks, feeling very left out of all the bustle.

As the afternoon drew to a close, Mildred crept downstairs and out into the darkening yard. She hurried to the pond and peered among the reeds to see if her friend was visible.

"Mr. Algernon, sir," she whispered, "come out, Mr. Algernon. I've got something to tell you, sir."

For a moment the water lay dark and still, then a ripple touched the surface and two green eyes appeared like periscopes.

"Oh, Mr. Algernon!" exclaimed Mildred with relief, and before he had time to hide away under a stone, as he usually did, she shot a hand into the water and scooped

him up. He did not want to be caught at all, and although Mildred told him where they were going and tried to soothe him, he struggled madly and looked at her with great suspicion. Mildred slid him carefully into her pocket and raced up the stairs to her room, where she transferred him to a small box with holes in the lid, which she had prepared specially for the journey.

"You'll be all right there for a while," she told him, tying on the lid with a piece of string. "You mustn't worry. It'll be all right—I promise."

The next step was to find and kidnap a suitable victim. Of course, the easiest thing to do would have been to change someone into a frog or snail or some other small creature which could easily be kept hidden in a box until she returned. But, to be honest, Mildred felt that there had been quite enough animal enchantments in the school to last a lifetime, and it seemed a less desperate measure to do a nice, straightforward kidnap, where at least you could see exactly what was happening.

As she came out of her room, Mildred saw a third-year witch named Griselda Blackwood approaching down the corridor, carrying her cat.

"Excuse me!" gasped Mildred. "Er—I was wondering if you could just come and help me for a moment?"

"Whatever for?" asked Griselda. "What's the matter, Mildred? You look quite pale."

"There's something horrible under my

bed!" exclaimed Mildred. "Could you come and help me get it out?"

"Something horrible?" repeated Griselda, drawing back in alarm. "Why, what do you mean *something horrible*? You can't really expect me to go fishing about underneath your bed if I don't even know what I might find under it, now can you?"

"It's a—er—beetle!" replied Mildred triumphantly. "I've got this *thing* about beetles. A horrid brown one with pincers ran up my pyjama leg once and I've never got over it. Please help me, Griselda. I won't get a wink of sleep otherwise."

"A beetle!" laughed Griselda. "Is that all? I thought it must be a tarantula at least with all the fuss you're making. Come on, then."

While Griselda was half under the bed, feeling about, Mildred very stealthily tied her bootlaces together.

"I can't seem to find anything," said Griselda, shuffling out and sitting back on her heels.

As quick as a flash, Mildred pulled out a lasso of rope which she had hidden in a drawer and slipped it over the astonished girl's head and shoulders, yanking it tightly enough to bind her arms to her sides. Before the poor victim had a chance to scream, Mildred had tied a gag around her mouth. As a last resort, Griselda tried to run for it, but of course her bootlaces were tied together, so she fell flat on her back.

"I'm really ever so sorry to do this to you," apologized Mildred humbly, as she tied Griselda's ankles together with her sash. "It's really in a very good cause and I'll explain everything to you later when I get back. I'm so sorry, I really am. I don't usually go around doing this sort of thing. I hope you don't mind *too* dreadfully."

Griselda stared up at Mildred from the floor with horror.

"Mmmmmmmmm!" she raged through the gag. "Mm-mmm, mmmm-mm, mm, mm, mm, mm, mmmm!"

Mildred pulled some bedclothes from her bed and covered Griselda tenderly.

"There really isn't any point in shouting," said Mildred, putting a pillow underneath the victim's head. "No one can hear you. They're all getting ready in the playground. I'll borrow your cat if you don't mind. Mine's awful on a broom, and anyway it's too easy to recognize."

Mildred changed from her ordinary school uniform to the best robes, which the girls always wore for special occasions. She unplaited her hair and shook it out loose. (The whole school, including the teachers, always wore their hair loose when they dressed in their best robes.) She put on her cape and turned up the collar and pulled her hat low over her eyes.

There was a soft "meeow" from the top of the wardrobe, and Mildred saw her little tabby cat watching reproachfully as she prepared to go without it.

"Oh, Tabby," said Mildred, reaching up and tickling its chin, "I can't take you or the whole school will recognize us."

She picked up the box with the frog magician in it and wedged it into her cape pocket. Then she slung Griselda's cat around her shoulders and took her broomstick from its place against the wall.

"Good-bye, Griselda," said Mildred, slinking out of the room feeling like a criminal. "I won't be long, and then I'll explain everything and you won't be cross anymore."

CHAPTER TEN

UT OF the window, as she hastened down the spiral staircase, Mildred saw the fires which were being lit in the ruins of the old castle where the celebrations were always held. Her heart pounded as she joined the throng of girls in the gloomy yard, all looking most dramatic with their hair loose and their long black robes and witches' hats.

"Thank goodness, it's almost dark," thought Mildred, tagging on to the end of form three as their form mistress counted them all.

"Is everyone accounted for?" asked Miss Cackle.

All the form mistresses answered "yes" in turn, and the pupils began their flight to the castle.

The school receded into the distance as the pupils skimmed above the treetops, and Mildred was grateful that no talking was allowed in flight, so nobody could ask her any awkward questions. The borrowed cat was a wonderful balancer, and Mildred felt rather disloyal as she found herself thinking how nice it would be to have a well-behaved sleek black cat which she could feel proud of.

Back at the academy, Ethel sat fuming in bed and watched from her window as the pupils rose like a flock of bats into the twilight and sailed away without her. She picked up her candle and decided to go

along to Mildred's room and have a grumble at her.

Outside Mildred's room, Ethel pressed her ear against the door and was surprised to hear a strange noise from within.

"Mildred?" called Ethel, knocking softly. The noise grew louder.

"Mmmmmm! Mmmm, mm, mmm!" Ethel opened the door and held up her candle to reveal the awful sight of Mildred's victim trussed up on the floor.

"What on earth has happened to you?" gasped Ethel, untying the gag and pulling at the knots in the sash and rope.

"It's that Mildred Hubble!" said Griselda, who was almost in tears. "She must have gone berserk. She got me in here under false pretences, tied me up, stole my cat, and went to the display in my place. Honestly, Ethel, she sounded really mad, wittering on about beetles up her pyjama leg and suchlike. Whatever shall we do?"

"Go after her, of course!" answered Ethel, delighted at the thought of the praise they would get when they revealed Mildred's wicked behaviour.

"Come on, Griselda, I'll change into my outdoor clothes and meet you in the yard with my broom in five minutes. We'll have to hurry. Goodness knows what that girl is planning!"

"All right," agreed Griselda. "I'll run and fetch my broom.

Meanwhile, the academy was alighting on the castle hillside and being welcomed by the chief magician and all the other witches and magicians. The chief magi-

cian, Mr. Hellibore, looked most imposing in his purple robe embroidered with moons and stars and a tall, pointed hat. Mildred would have been absolutely thrilled by it all if she had not been so terrified of the task ahead of her.

There was a long delay between the pupils' arrival and the commencement of the displays and chanting, during which Miss Cackle and the teachers greeted friends and acquaintances, and the girls all stood to attention, being neat and well behaved and a credit to the school.

Suddenly there was a commotion in the sky, and everyone looked up to see Ethel and Griselda swooping down on their brooms, waving and shouting.

"Mildred Hubble's down there!" shrieked Ethel.

"She kidnapped me!" yelled Griselda. "And she tied me up, so she could come in my place!"

"That's enough now, girls, thank you," ordered Miss Cackle, who was not at all pleased at such unseemly shrieking from her girls.

Miss Hardbroom strode across to the rows of pupils, and Mildred pulled her hat even lower over her face. From under the brim she could see the chief magician nearby, looking rather puzzled at all the shouting.

"If you *are* here, Mildred," said Miss Hardbroom, "I would advise you to step forward at *once* and explain yourself."

The pupils all began looking round at each other, and Mildred knew there was little time before someone recognized her. There was no alternative but to make a dash to the magician before anyone could catch her. Summoning every scrap of courage, Mildred suddenly barged through the rows of pupils and threw herself in front of Mr. Hellibore.

"Please forgive me, Your Honour," she said, thrusting the box containing her friend into his hands. "I know you didn't want me to come here tonight, but there

is an enchanted magician in that box and I promised him that I would get him to you so that you could change him back. I'm so sorry to cause such a lot of trouble, but I didn't know what else to do."

"What on earth is all this nonsense about?" asked the chief magician sternly. "And are my eyes deceiving me or are you not the girl who *ruined* the broomstick display last year? If so—"

"We do apologize most humbly, Your Honour," grovelled Miss Hardbroom, seizing Mildred's arm in a vice-like grip. "The girl seems to have taken leave of her senses—"

"I *haven't*, Miss Hardbroom!" interrupted Mildred. "*Please*, Your Honour, Mr. Hellibore, sir, it really *is* a magician. His name is Algernon Webb-something, Stonely-Webb, oh *something* like that, only he couldn't quite remember. He's been a frog for simply ages."

"Good gracious me!" exclaimed Mr. Hellibore. "Do you know, Miss Hardbroom, it might just be Algernon Rowan-Webb. He was my roommate in the days when your school was used as a sort of summer camp for magicians, and he actually *did* disappear one day and we all thought he must have gone home. But it was *decades* ago — why, the poor chap! If you'll excuse me, Miss Hardbroom."

Mildred kept her eyes firmly closed as the chief magician opened the box and intoned the release spell. Suddenly there was a gasp from the crowd. Mildred opened her eyes and breathed a huge sigh of relief.

Standing in front of them was an extremely old man with a beard that trailed on the ground and long flowing white hair. He was very bent over and was rubbing his eyes as if he couldn't quite believe it.

"*Algy*, old chap!" exclaimed the chief

magician with joy. "It's *Egbert,* your old friend. Don't you remember?"

"Egbert!" replied Algernon. "Yes, of course I remember, though you were a lot younger in those days. Excuse me a moment; I shall have to sit down. It's all a bit much for me after all these years as a frog. My legs and arms feel awfully cramped. Egbert Hellibore! Well, well, what a piece of luck."

"The luck came from your little friend here," said Mr. Hellibore, placing a hand on Mildred's shoulder. "This child braved all our displeasure to bring you here."

Mildred felt very shy as the vast crowd fell silent and every pair of eyes swivelled in her direction.

"Do you remember me, Mr. Rowan-Webb, sir?" asked Mildred. "We were frogs together."

"*Remember* you?" repeated Algernon. "My dear Mildred, how could I ever forget you? No one ever had a truer friend. Without your help I would have been a frog forever. And please call me Algernon."

"Well, Miss Hardbroom," said Mr. Hellibore, "we can hardly send the girl back to school again after this act of heroism, now can we?"

Miss Hardbroom ground her teeth and managed a horribly false smile. "Whatever you wish, Your Honour," she replied.

"Is there anything you would like as a reward, my child?" asked Mr. Hellibore, smiling kindly down at Mildred.

Mildred thought for a moment. "Oh, yes, sir!" she replied. "There *is* one thing."

She stepped forward on tiptoe and whispered in his ear.

"Is that *all*?" said Mr. Hellibore with a laugh. He leaned across and quietly told the ancient magician what Mildred had asked for. Algernon smiled dreamily. "What a wonderful memory you have, my dear," he said. "Yes, that would be very nice, very nice indeed."

The crowd watched in fascinated silence as Mr. Hellibore snapped his fingers and a small table appeared in his hand, set with a white tablecloth, tea for three, and a huge plate of toast, crumpets, and butter. Algernon peered at the table, then snapped *his* fingers and a pot of honey appeared. "Mustn't forget *that*," he commented as he set it on the table. And, with a glow of pride, Mildred walked away arm-in-arm with the two most important people at the celebrations, to have a proper old-fashioned tea by the nearest bonfire.

THE
Worst Witch
AT SEA

TO CHLOE AND ALICE WITH LOVE FOREVER

CHAPTER ONE

A VIOLENT snowstorm greeted the pupils of Miss Cackle's Academy for Witches as they returned to school for the first day of the Summer Term.

There were two terms dividing the school year: the Winter Term, which began in September, continuing until January, and the Summer Term, which began in March, ending in July. With five solid months to each term, you can imagine how bleak it felt during the middle months, when every minute seemed like an hour, with no light flickering at the end of the tunnel.

The girls were used to appalling weather for the first few weeks of the Summer Term because it was so early in the year, but this time it had surpassed itself.

Miss Cackle, the kindly headmistress of the school, watched from her study window as the pupils arrived in ones and twos, battling to stay on their broomsticks, cloaks turned inside out and summer dresses flapping wildly in the screaming wind.

Mildred Hubble, a second-year, already renowned as the worst witch in the school, lurched out of the yellow-grey clouds with a crust of snow covering her broomstick, cat, suitcase, and summer dress, which was a new design this year.

Miss Hardbroom (Mildred's horrifically strict form mistress) had decided that the

old design of black and grey checks was too frivolous for the girls and had persuaded the headmistress to have them replaced with nice, sensible, plain black. Miss Cackle had meekly agreed with Miss Hardbroom's plan as she usually did (being a person who always avoided any trouble), but she had secretly rather liked the old uniform. The whole business had caused much merriment among the girls, who could scarcely believe that anyone, even Miss Hardbroom, could consider black and grey checks and grey ankle socks to be frivolous.

Mildred wondered if she was actually frozen onto her broomstick as she struggled to steer it over the wall and into the yard. She turned to check that her tabby cat was still with her, as the poor creature was terrified of flying at the best of times and had been yowling his head off for the whole journey. He was, but as they cleared the top of the gates by inches, the little cat attempted to jump off, causing Mildred to crash-land into a deep snowdrift which curved in an elegant arc against one of the broomstick sheds. It was quite sheltered

in the yard, and Mildred lay in the snow getting her breath back, watching the other pupils coming in to land, most of them more successfully than herself.

"You are a pain, T-T-Tabby," said Mildred, her teeth chattering with cold. "How am I ever going to get anywhere in this place while I'm st-t-tuck with a cat like you?"

Tabby shook himself, and snow sprayed over Mildred's already snow-covered face. She even had icicles hanging from the brim of her hat, and Tabby's fur stood out in little frozen peaks. They made a sorry pair.

"Maud, is that you?" Mildred called out, as a hunched bundle of broomstick and baggage wobbled over the wall and glided into the snow a few yards away.

"Millie!" yelled a voice which was unmistakably that of her best friend. "Incredible weather, isn't it? And they call it *Summer* Term!"

Mildred scrambled to her feet, brushed off as much snow as she could and waded across to Maud, dragging her suitcase and broomstick behind her. Tabby had now assumed his usual position, draped around Mildred's shoulders like a fur stole.

"Do you think they might light a few fires as a special concession?" asked Mildred.

"I shouldn't think so," said Maud. "You know what they're like—healthy fresh air at all times. What about the uniform, then? Frivolous! I ask you!"

The yard was rapidly filling up with pupils, all stamping their feet to warm themselves and hoping that they might be allowed inside instead of assembling in the yard as usual. They made a rather dramatic sight dotted about like crows against the glaring white.

The main door opened and Ethel Hallow, a member of Mildred's class generally known for her bossiness, especially towards Mildred, appeared with a note, which she pinned to the door.

The note read:

NO ONE is allowed inside without permission. Girls must assemble in lines in the yard. When the bell rings, they should proceed to the cloak-rooms in single file to deposit their bags and from there proceed to morning assembly in the Great Hall.

"I *told* you," said Maud grimly. "And how did Ethel get inside when we're all out here? That's what *I'd* like to know. Look at her, all dry and comfortable when everyone else is frozen stiff, waiting to be summoned out of the storm."

"Watch out, Maud," said Mildred. "She's beckoning to us."

"Mildred Hubble," shouted Ethel from the shelter of the doorway, "Miss Cackle wants to see you in her study straightaway. Didn't take you long this time, did it?" She couldn't resist sneering. "How many minutes have you been here—five, is it?"

She pulled a face and ducked inside, closing the door behind her.

"Oh, Maud," said Mildred. "Miss Cackle must have seen me crash-landing. You'd think she'd have let me off a bit, with a force nine gale and a blizzard going on."

"Never mind, Mil," comforted Maud. "I wish she wanted to see *me*. There'll be a fire roaring in her study, and at least you'll be able to warm up. Anyway, I'll bet it's not even about your crash-landing— probably something perfectly pleasant."

"Perfectly pleasant!" giggled Mildred. "Well, I'd better go and find out what I've done. Why don't you see if you can find Enid while I'm in there? She must have arrived by now."

Enid was their other friend.

"Good idea," said Maud. "Best of luck, then."

Mildred gathered up her suitcase and broom and made her way up the snow-clad stone steps and in through the heavy front door.

CHAPTER TWO

T WASN'T much warmer inside the school than out in the snow-swept yard. There was no glass in the castle-style windows, and there were little drifts of snow in regular heaps beneath the window ledges all the way along the corridor. Miss Cackle's door loomed ahead and Mildred slowed to a snail's pace to put off the moment when she would have to enter and see what she had done now, ten minutes after the start of term.

She knocked very softly, hoping that she might not be heard.

"Come in!" called Miss Cackle's cheery voice from inside. Mildred pushed open the door, and there was Miss Cackle sitting at her desk with a glorious log fire blazing in the grate.

"Ah, Mildred, my dear," continued Miss Cackle. "Come and sit here by the fire; you look absolutely frozen. I want to have a little chat with you. Ghastly weather, isn't it?"

"Yes, Miss Cackle," agreed Mildred politely, feeling less anxious as she noted the good-humoured tone of Miss Cackle's voice. Perhaps it *was* something "perfectly pleasant" after all, as Maud had said.

Mildred sat down gratefully in a chair next to the hearth, and Tabby jumped down from her shoulders and curled up so near the grate that his fur almost caught fire.

"Tabby!" called Mildred, clicking her fingers. "Come back here at once."

But the little cat was too intent on thawing out to obey his mistress's orders. Also thawing out were the icicles on Mildred's hat, and three of them descended simultaneously to the floor with a gentle clinking sound.

"Now then, Mildred," said Miss Cackle, pressing her fingertips together and surveying Mildred over the top of them. "I wanted to speak to you about that little cat of yours. Sweet, isn't he?"

"Oh, yes, Miss Cackle," said Mildred. "He's *very* sweet. Not very *good*. I mean I can't get him to do anything right and he's still petrified of flying, but he's very good-natured and—"

"Yes, dear," said Miss Cackle. "I can see that he's a charming little cat, but I was watching your arrival just now and I couldn't help noticing that you were pulled off balance by the cat as you came over the gates. He really is a rather useless

creature, despite his nice nature, and he *looks* terrible, too, when we're all on display—hanging on by his claws, spread out flat, when all the other cats are sitting up nice and straight by now—except for the first years' kittens, of course. Yours has never really got past the kitten phase, has he, my dear? And of course he has completely the wrong markings for the school and looks very untidy next to the black ones."

Mildred stared at Miss Cackle, a wave of alarm spreading through her. Another icicle broke from her hat and fell into her lap.

"Anyway, dear," Miss Cackle continued. "I was wondering if a more normal, regulation black cat might possibly help you with your studies. One of the third-year girls, Fenella Feverfew, transferred to Miss Pentangle's Academy last term and left behind her extremely well-trained cat— they have owls at Miss Pentangle's, so she had no use for a cat. *You* could have it if you like."

Mildred was appalled. She scooped Tabby from the hearth and clutched him to her damp, unfrivolous summer dress, the remaining icicles tinkling on to the floor as she did so.

"But what about Tabby, Miss Cackle!" she exclaimed. "I mean, it's very kind of you to consider me like this, but I've had him now for nearly two years and he depends on me—especially as he isn't very clever, and I'm very fond of him."

Miss Cackle smiled indulgently at Mildred, who looked rather appealing standing in a puddle of melted snow, her clothes and plaits dripping wet, with the pathetic little cat clasped to her heart.

"Now then, dear," she said. "There's nothing to worry about. Miss Tapioca, the school cook, was only telling me this morning that the kitchen is having a mouse problem and that she needs a good mouser. I would say that little Tabby here is just right for the job, wouldn't you? And it won't matter about his stripes, tucked away out of sight down in the kitchen."

"But, Miss Cackle," said Mildred, "Tabby's frightened of mice. He doesn't—"

"Nonsense, Mildred," laughed Miss Cackle. "No cat is afraid of mice! What an idea. No, I think your work will improve no end if you accept my offer of Fenella's cat. And Tabby will have the time of his life down in the kitchen chasing mice all day and curling up by the range when he's tired. Off you go now. Miss Tapioca is expecting you—I rang her a moment ago. Run along, dear, or you'll be late for assembly. Miss Tapioca has Tabby's re-placement in a basket downstairs."

"Yes, Miss Cackle. Thank you, Miss Cackle," said Mildred, trying unsuccessfully not to cry. She held Tabby even tighter and went out into the corridor, where the icy wind struck her in the face as she left the warm fireside behind her and closed the door.

CHAPTER THREE

THE KITCHEN was in the basement of the school. It was reached by several long, dark corridors and narrow staircases. It took about half an hour to get there from the dining hall, which explained why the food was always stone cold.

"Now, don't be scared, Tabby," Mildred

sobbed into the little cat's rumpled fur. "I'll work out a plan to get you back with me again. I'll sneak down and give you extra training sessions so you'll get better at flying, and perhaps I could make you a little black coat to hide the stripes. I don't know why they're being so funny about that now, after all this time. *They* gave you to me in the first place. It's not fair."

There was great activity in the kitchen, which, because of its gigantic range, was mercifully warm. Over the range bubbled huge cauldrons of the atrocious porridge to be served for the girls' breakfast, after assembly.

Mildred stood unnoticed in the doorway watching the four undercooks charging about. Miss Tapioca, a large person, proportioned very much like a cottage loaf, with white hair bundled into a hairnet, sat at one end of the fifteen-foot-long kitchen table looking up a recipe.

"Ah, Mildred Hubble!" she said, glancing up and seeing the bedraggled Mildred lurking in the shadows. "Have you brought our new mouser? Come and show it to us, girl. Don't just stand there staring."

Mildred brought Tabby out from beneath her cloak and held him up. The

four undercooks had gathered round as well and they all tickled him on top of his head and smoothed his wind-blown fur.

"Just right for a mouser," said Miss Tapioca. "And here is Ebony in exchange. Much too intelligent and well trained to be wasted in the kitchen. Well, put the cat down, Mildred—unless you want to stay with him and catch mice yourself?"

She handed Mildred the basket. Mildred could see a pair of brilliant green eyes

gazing at her from the shadow inside. Tabby, nicely warmed up by the hot kitchen, had retreated to his favourite position round Mildred's neck. There was nothing else to be done, except to take the basket and go.

"May I come and visit him?" asked Mildred, her voice quivering as she un-curled Tabby from her neck and placed him in Miss Tapioca's arms.

"I don't think that would be very sensible,

Mildred," said Miss Tapioca, holding Tabby in a very tight grip as the little cat was grimly trying to get back onto Mildred's shoulders. "He will be much too busy chasing mice to spare any time for visitors. Off you go and take care of Ebony—now that really *is* a cat to be proud of. You'll forget this little scruff in five minutes once you've been out flying with a cat like Ebony. Listen! There's the bell for assembly. You'd better hurry."

Mildred left the kitchen without looking back. She could hear Tabby yowling desperately as he tried to follow her. She dived up the stairs two at a time, ran to her room, dumped her suitcase, broomstick, and the cat basket, and sprinted the last few corridors to join Maud and Enid marching into the Great Hall.

"Hello, Mil," said Enid. "What's wrong?"

"What's the matter, Mildred?" asked Maud. "You look as if something ghastly's happened."

"It has," said Mildred, bursting into tears as quietly as possible, bearing in mind the fact that they were on their way into assembly. "I'll tell you about it later."

After assembly, during which Miss Cackle announced that lunch break would be in the Great Hall instead of the yard because the snow was already several feet thick, the girls trooped off to their form rooms, to be greeted by their form mistresses.

Mildred's form were unfortunate enough to be presided over by Miss Hardbroom, the most terrifying mistress in the school. She was a genius at reducing her pupils to a gibbering heap with one withering glance. No one ever dreamed of passing a note, or giggling, or even speaking, unless asked a question, during Miss Hardbroom's lessons.

On the way to class, Mildred managed to tell Enid and Maud the sad news about Tabby.

Miss Hardbroom was sitting bolt upright behind her desk, waiting for the girls to settle, as they all filed into the room and took their places, arranging books and writing equipment in their desks. The room was only fractionally warmer than outside, and the girls discreetly rubbed their feet and blew on their hands in a futile attempt to warm themselves up.

"Come along now, girls," said Miss Hardbroom. "Stop all this silly nonsense. It isn't *that* cold. Lunch break isn't far away, and then you can all run briskly around the Great Hall to get yourselves nice and warm. Anyway, girls, welcome back for the Summer Term—Mildred Hubble, what is the matter *now*?"

Mildred looked at her feet, embarrassed by the tears which she could not stop from rolling down her cheeks.

"It's her cat, Miss Hardbroom," said Maud. "Miss Cackle sent it to be a kitchen mouser, and Mildred's got Fenella Feverfew's, because Fenella left it behind when she left last term."

"Well, Mildred," said Miss Hardbroom, "I don't know what you are crying for. I would have seen it more as a cause for celebration if I were you. Fenella's cat is an absolute credit to the school. I hope we shall soon see a marked improvement in your flying, without that nuisance of a tabby. Sit down and pull yourself together at once.

"I have an announcement to make, girls," she continued, "which should cheer Mildred up considerably. Mr. Rowan-Webb, the magician Mildred rescued from the school pond last term, has written and asked if Mildred and her form would like to spend a week at his home by the sea during the Summer Term, by way of a thank-you to Mildred."

There were gasps of delight from the girls, who all turned to Mildred with joyous comments.

"It seems that we all have *you* to thank for this little treat," said Miss Hardbroom, making it sound as if Mildred had done something wrong.

Mildred didn't know whether to smile or look solemn.

"Goodness me, girl," said Miss Hardbroom, noting Mildred's anxious face. "Surely the thought of a week at the seaside is a cheering thought?"

"Oh, yes, Miss Hardbroom," sniffed Mildred, "it's cheered me up very much. But I was wondering if I could bring Tabby with me as a little break from the kitchen. I wondered if it would . . ." Her voice trailed away as she saw Miss Hardbroom's eyebrow arch into a slant, like a poised spear.

There was no point in continuing. Mildred stared down at her feet and tried to look suitably pleased about the holiday, which was difficult when trying not to cry.

Maud sneaked a hand under Mildred's desk and squeezed her friend's arm. They both knew that a holiday would be no fun at all with Tabby left behind in the kitchen wondering why Mildred didn't come to collect him.

CHAPTER FOUR

GRADUALLY, the weather improved. It stopped snowing, the snow melted, and soon the girls were all out in the chilly playground again, trying to devise new ways of keeping warm. The holiday was planned for the first week in May and everyone hoped that it might be warm enough by then to swim and have some fun. Mildred was the only one who didn't seem to be looking forward to the treat in any way.

"I wonder if there'll be a sandy beach," said Maud, as they all stood ankle-deep in slush in the playground during lunch break.

"—and caves!" said Enid.

"And a whole week of sunshine so that we can sunbathe and swim," said Maud. "What do *you* think, Mil?"

"Mildred *doesn't* think," said Ethel Hallow, who just happened to be passing by on her way to the library. "At least, I didn't see much evidence of any thought last term."

"Oh, do leave me alone, Ethel," said Mildred, hunching her cloak up around her ears.

"Not looking forward to our little treat, then?" Ethel continued in her usual sneering tone. "I can't think why the whole thing's in honour of *you,* anyway. You're always messing everything up. You're the worst witch in the school—"

"Come on, Mildred," said Maud, trying to keep the peace. "Let's go somewhere else and leave Ethel to her sour grapes."

They all trailed across the playground

and tried to get out of the wind by huddling in the broom shed (which is exactly the same as a bike shed, except that it houses broomsticks instead of bicycles).

In fact, Ethel's observations about the holiday in Mildred's honour were very ill-advised. The whole incident ending up with Mildred in the pond had been completely due to Ethel in the first place. During the Winter Term, Ethel had changed Mildred into a frog. Mildred had hopped off to find help and been discovered by Miss Hardbroom, who had put her into a jar in the potion laboratory. The frog-Mildred had escaped from her jar and fled to the pond to hide, where she had met the magician, Mr. Rowan-Webb, also turned into a frog by enchantment. Mildred had rescued him and made sure he was reinstated as a human, so he was naturally very grateful to her, but Ethel was jealous of all the attention and praise which had been heaped on Mildred.

"What's up, Mil?" asked Maud. "Aren't you even a *bit* thrilled about the holiday? Miss Hardbroom's already sent off for our regulation swimming costumes and bathing hats. I think it's the most exciting thing that's happened for years."

"Sorry to be a wet blanket, Maud," said Mildred. "I'm just a bit fed up at the moment, that's all."

"Don't worry, Mil," said Enid. "I'm sure you'll be just as glad as everyone else by the time we actually set off to—where is it? What's the name of the place where the magician lives?"

"Gloom Castle, Grim Cove," said Mildred.

"What a terrible name!" said Enid.

"You're joking!" exclaimed Maud.

"No, I'm not," said Mildred. "I saw it at the top of the letter on Miss Hardbroom's

desk. Sounds brilliant, doesn't it? I can just see us all frozen to death, doing broomstick practice up and down 500-foot sheer cliffs in our swimming costumes—anyway, just imagine what the swimming costumes will be like! If Miss Hardbroom thought our black and grey checked dresses were frivolous, goodness knows what she'll come up with for swimwear. Anyway, I'm bound to get everything wrong. Ethel's right, really— I *do* mess everything up. I *am* the worst witch in the school."

Maud and Enid felt awful. Mildred was truly down in the dumps, and nothing they could say seemed to cheer her up. What they didn't know was that she had another secret fear—like her embarrassing fear of the dark. Mildred couldn't swim. She had never learned how to, and even with armbands or a ring around her middle she was as terrified as Tabby on the back of the broomstick.

Tabby was the other problem. She missed Tabby so dreadfully that nothing could make her feel better—nothing except having Tabby back again—and she didn't know how to work out a plan to rescue him.

Ebony, Fenella's cat, was a first-rate cat, almost as good as Ethel's. Mildred felt a twinge of disloyalty as she zoomed around the playground during broomstick practice

with the perfectly trained Ebony bolt upright behind her. It really *was* a help to
have a cat which was a credit to you. But
at night, Ebony would set off through the
window and along the school wall for a
night of hunting, whereas dear, scruffy
old Tabby had always spent the night
curled up either on Mildred's chest or
round the top of her head like a fur hat.
Enid gave Mildred a rather nice furry

tabby-cat hot-water bottle, but it only made her feel worse.

If only someone had invented a hot-water bottle that purred, thought Mildred sadly, as she curled up under the bed-clothes in the dark.

CHAPTER FIVE

EVERY so often, Mildred made secret trips to the kitchen in an attempt to visit her abandoned pet. However, the kitchen was always bustling with cooks and dinner ladies, and so far she had only caught one glimpse of Tabby, looking rather thin and even more motheaten than usual, curled up on top of a tall cupboard in a dark corner. Each time, someone had noticed Mildred skulking in the shadows and shooed her away.

Meanwhile, the holiday at Grim Cove loomed nearer. One morning, Miss Hardbroom strode into the classroom with a large box containing the swimwear so eagerly awaited by Mildred's class.

Their spirits sank as Miss Hardbroom held up one of the costumes for their inspection. It was like one of those old-fashioned Victorian bathing costumes, in black and grey stripes, with elbow-length sleeves and knee-length legs. The school badge, depicting a black cat on a yellow moon, was embroidered across the chest, and to crown this outfit was a close-fitting black swimming hat.

Miss Hardbroom narrowed her eyes as her glance darted around the room.

"Well, girls," she said coldly, "I *had* hoped for slightly more enthusiasm from all of you. Miss Cackle has gone to considerable trouble and expense to kit you out with these superb garments. In fact,

Miss Cackle has decided to join us for our exciting week on holiday. Isn't that wonderful? The remainder of the lesson will be spent making cards for Miss Cackle, to thank her for your marvellous swimming outfits."

A faint groan of general disappointment rumbled around the classroom like distant thunder, as they all heaved open their desk lids and rummaged around for their coloured pencils.

That evening, the members of Form
Two all tried on their swimming costumes
in the washroom before they got into their

nightclothes. Mildred's was slightly too
large and rather baggy, and Maud's was
unfortunately a little too tight, so that the
school badge was stretched sideways
across her front. Needless to say, Ethel's
fitted like a glove and even managed to
look quite smart.

"I have four cups for swimming from the first school I attended," said Ethel. "We had a huge swimming-pool there and I won cups for everything—diving, lifesaving, relay racing, and broomstick water-skiing."

"Gosh," said Mildred. "What's broom-stick water-skiing?"

"Don't you know *anything*, Mildred Hubble?" said Ethel in her infuriatingly superior tone. "It's easy-peasy. You have skis on both feet, like ordinary skis, then you tie a piece of rope to the back of your broom, and off you zoom, holding on to the rope so the broomstick pulls you along like a boat. We can have races at Grim Cove. Of course, *I'll* win, but it's jolly good fun, even for all the losers."

Mildred wondered if she ought to confess to Maud that she couldn't swim, but it was so depressing constantly being hopeless at everything. She longed to say to everyone, "Oh, yes, I'm brilliant at such and such. Let me help you," instead of spending her whole life desperately trying to memorize spells in the library and ending up in Miss Cackle's study explaining for the hundredth time why everything had gone wrong.

Also brewing in the back of Mildred's mind was a plan to kidnap (or catnap) Tabby from the kitchen and smuggle him away on the holiday with them. Even if she got into the most awful trouble on their return, she felt it would be worth it to spend a whole week with her much-loved pet, and she really did want to enjoy the holiday, particularly as it was a result of one thing that she had actually done right—saving Mr. Rowan-Webb, the kindly old magician, from a lifetime of frogdom.

"Are you *up* to something, Mil?" asked Enid one evening at dinner.

"Yes," said Maud. "You've got that faraway, vague sort of look you get when you're thinking up some scheme or other."

"What?" asked Mildred vaguely, glancing up from a ghastly-looking plate of grey stew with a slab of yellow cabbage in the middle.

"I *told* you," said Enid. "She's *up* to something."

"No, I'm not," said Mildred. "And I'm really starting to look forward to the holiday now. I think we're all going to have a very exciting time."

"Not too exciting, Mildred," said Maud uneasily. "We don't want any trouble, do we?"

But Mildred wasn't listening. She was busily working out the finer details of her plan to snatch Tabby twenty minutes before takeoff on their broomsticks for the flight to Grim Cove.

CHAPTER SIX

LUCK WAS on Mildred's side for once. Miss Cackle announced that the journey to the magician's castle would begin at dawn. Each girl would have a packed breakfast to eat halfway through the journey, which would be ready and stowed away in their suitcase the night before. Miss Cackle also announced that, as it was a fairly long flight, lasting two hours, all pupils' cats would be transported in cat baskets to save any accidents with sleepy or nervous cats falling off into the treetops below.

This meant that firstly the kitchen staff would not be up and about and secondly there would be a conveniently dark cat basket in which to hide Tabby.

Mildred did consider telling Maud and Enid of her plan, but she knew that they would be so anxious on her behalf that it would only worry them, so she decided against it.

The morning of the holiday dawned. Mildred had been up and dressed for two hours, hoping that Ebony would be back early from his night out hunting, as he was sometimes out until long after dawn. Thankfully, on this occasion, he was back twenty minutes before the first blush of morning light stole across the cloudy, grey sky.

Mildred seized the elegant black creature as he positioned himself ready to spring from the window ledge onto the top of the wardrobe. She bundled him

into the cat basket and crept out into the deserted corridor.

There was a dim night-lantern burning at the end of each corridor and at the head of each staircase, so she was easily able to make her way to the kitchen, once her eyes had adjusted to the gloomy light.

The kitchen looked strange with no one in it, all the pots and pans hanging on their hooks and no fires burning in the cooking ranges. The only sign of life was the pattering of dozens of tiny feet as mice swarmed all over the tables and worktops looking for leftover crumbs. Obviously Tabby was no use whatsoever in his new job.

"Tabby," called Mildred softly. A shiver ran down her spine as she peered around into all the dark corners, huge creepy-looking cauldrons and storage cupboards with doors half open as if someone might be lurking inside.

"Tab!" she called again. "It's me. It's Mildred. I've come to fetch you."

One of the cupboard doors creaked open and Mildred screamed, her heart banging in her ears with fright.

An answering "Miaow!" set her mind at rest as Tabby came pattering softly to greet her, a half-eaten kipper dangling out of his mouth. The little cat was so delighted to see his mistress that he dropped the kipper and leaped into her arms, where there was much miaowing and cuddling, and even weeping from Mildred.

Tabby settled contentedly around Mildred's neck as if to say, "Now, where *have* you been all this time?" and Mildred bent down and unlatched the cat basket.

Ebony stalked out looking rather annoyed at being shoved into the basket and then unceremoniously plonked out onto the cold, stone kitchen floor.

"Off you go, Eb," whispered Mildred. "I'm taking Tabby for a little holiday, so you can stand in for him while he's away. Oh, Tabby, they're all going to go *mad* when they find out. Perhaps they won't notice, with a bit of luck. Still I don't care. It's worth *anything* to have you back, even for a week. Come on, you'll have to go into the basket or we'll be found out before we even get there."

Tabby didn't mind going into the basket at all. Mildred could hear him purring like a car engine as she headed for the kitchen door. As she heaved it open, several mice skittered out from beneath the large table and dived past into the corridor, pursued by Ebony.

Mildred giggled, "Oh, Tabby," she said, scratching his head fondly through the wicker bars. "You're such a hopeless case. I *have* missed you."

CHAPTER SEVEN

OPERATION Rescue Tabby had taken longer than Mildred had calculated, and she arrived in the yard to find everyone, including Miss Cackle and Miss Hardbroom, all lined up and ready to set off. They were standing in rows, in absolute silence, as Mildred burst through the main door and clumped to her place in line.

"Ah, Mildred," said Miss Hardbroom crisply. "How kind of you to join us. Perhaps you had a little problem getting up so early in the morning?"

"Yes, Miss Hardbroom," agreed Mildred, relieved to be provided with an excuse. "And then I had to wait for Ebony to come in from his hunting and then I couldn't get him to go into the basket and *then* I couldn't . . ."

"That will do, Mildred!" snapped Miss Hardbroom. "I really don't want to stand here all morning listening to a never-ending list of all the things you couldn't do before we were graced with your presence. Now then, if Miss Cackle is agreeable, we shall proceed to Grim Cove and the splendid holiday which awaits us."

Miss Cackle smiled and nodded at the girls. "Most certainly, Miss Hardbroom," she said. "Let us proceed at once! We don't want to waste one moment of our jolly holiday, do we, girls?"

Form Two let out a loud cheer of agreement.

"That is quite enough, girls!" exclaimed Miss Hardbroom. "Miss Cackle doesn't want to be deafened. Now, Mildred Hubble, a word in your ear. Mr. Rowan-Webb has kindly bestowed this holiday upon Form Two out of gratitude for your helpful action in saving him from the pond. He obviously thinks most highly of you, so let us hope that you will not do anything whatsoever to disillusion him. Do you think you can manage an entire week without drawing any unwanted attention to yourself? In other words, Mildred, no silly nonsense—all right?"

"Oh, definitely, Miss Hardbroom," said Mildred, feeling distinctly nervous as she held the cat basket containing the wrong cat underneath her cloak.

"Good," said Miss Hardbroom. "Then let us depart. Ethel, dear, lead on. Follow the river.

The girls commanded their broomsticks
to hover and hooked their suitcases and
cat baskets over the twigs at the back. Then
they all arranged themselves sidesaddle,
jammed their hats on as firmly as possible,
and took hold of their broomsticks—
some more grimly than others. Ethel sat
as upright as a telegraph pole, her fingers

loosely curled around the stick. At the other end of the scale, Mildred was hanging on so tightly that her knuckles were white and she was almost bent double.

Ethel led the class over the wall and down the mountain towards the shining river, which was like a mauve and pink ribbon in the sunrise.

"Gosh, Maud," said Mildred. "It looks really beautiful at this time of day, doesn't it? Perhaps we'll have wonderful weather and it *will* be a great holiday after all."

"It won't be if your cat doesn't shut up," said Maud, looking back at Mildred's cat basket, from whence a desperate yowling had just started.

Ethel swooped back alongside Mildred. "There's something *about* you, Mildred Hubble, isn't there?" she observed unpleasantly. "I mean, even a superb cat like

Ebony goes berserk the moment it falls into your clutches. Perhaps being worst at everything is catching—you know, like measles."

She zoomed ahead again to take her place as leader of the form.

Miss Hardbroom and Miss Cackle were in front of everyone and Mildred heard Ethel say, "I just went to see if Mildred's cat was all right, Miss Hardbroom. Any cat of hers seems to become nervous of flying—even one like Ebony."

"Thank you, Ethel," said Miss Hardbroom. "Most thoughtful of you, my dear . . . Mildred!" she called over her shoulder into the wind. "What on earth is the matter with Ebony?"

Tabby was scrabbling at the basket and miaowing at the top of his voice.

"He ate rather a large mouse, Miss Hardbroom," replied Mildred. "I don't think he's feeling very well."

"We'll take a look at him when we land for our breakfast," Miss Hardbroom called back.

Mildred was horrified. They had not even arrived at Grim Cove and she had already got herself into the most awful trouble. One glimpse of Tabby, and Miss Hardbroom would probably expel her on the spot, holiday or no holiday.

CHAPTER EIGHT

AFTER AN hour of flying, everyone was beginning to feel exhausted and hungry. Although the sun had risen into a perfectly blue sky, the wind was cold so high up, and Tabby's desperate complaining was beginning to grate on everyone's nerves.

Miss Cackle and Miss Hardbroom signalled to the girls to begin their descent to an area where a loop of river passed through a wood with a large shingle bank on either side of the water.

"Breakfast at last!" whispered Maud to Mildred. "I'm starving."

Mildred wasn't listening. She was wondering how to get out of having Tabby examined by Miss Hardbroom.

"Land at the shingle bank!" called Miss Hardbroom, as they descended like a flock of birds into the woodland. "Only a quarter of an hour for our break, girls. We must press on as soon as possible."

Miss Cackle and Miss Hardbroom landed perfectly, followed by Ethel and the rest of Form Two, all except Mildred.

Tabby finally stopped yowling as he and Mildred fell off into a dense thicket several yards from the landing place.

"I'm sorry, Miss Hardbroom," Mildred's voice called apologetically from the middle of the bushes. "There's so much on the back of my broom, I think I must have put too much into my suitcase. At least Tab . . . Ebony's stopped making such a noise. He looks much better now, what I can see of him in the gloom. I seem to be a bit stuck."

"Shall I go and help her, Miss Hard-broom?" asked Maud.

"No, Maud," said Miss Hardbroom wearily. She turned in the direction of Mildred's bush. "Just stay where you are, Mildred. I think the sight of you would put me off my breakfast at this moment. We'll pull you out when we set off again."

Mildred breathed a sigh of relief as she wedged herself into the branches of a rather prickly bush and rummaged in her suitcase for her package of sandwiches.

"It worked, Tab!" she whispered. "They've forgotten about you. Now *please* calm down for the rest of the journey. I might break my neck if I have to make myself crash a second time! Look, Tab, they're tuna sand-wiches; you can have some if you like. I don't think you'll be too keen on apple juice though."

For a while there was no sound except the birds singing and the rustling of paper bags as the girls demolished their food. Somehow, whenever Miss Hardbroom was present, no one ever dared to speak, although they were allowed to chat during mealtimes provided the noise didn't get too loud.

"Ethel," said Miss Hardbroom, as they tidied away the breakfast things, "would you kindly assist Mildred in her plight among the bushes so that we may continue on our journey?"

Ethel bustled about self-importantly, attaching a rope to the back of her broomstick. Then she took off on the broom with a lasso of rope over her arm, rather like a cowboy, and called to Mildred to get ready.

Mildred arranged her suitcase and cat basket over the back of the broom and caught the rope, while Ethel hovered overhead. In fact, Ethel dropped the rope onto Mildred's head so abruptly that it nearly knocked her out.

"Whoops!" said Ethel. "Silly me! Are you ready, Mildred? One, two, three, UP!" And she sped off at forty miles per hour, while Mildred, plus broom and baggage, was jerked into the air flat out at the end of the rope, hanging on for dear life.

"Thank you, Ethel!" called Miss Cackle, who was watching with Miss Hardbroom. "That will do, dear. Mildred is well clear of the bushes now.

Fortunately, Tabby seemed less hysterical for the second half of the journey. Perhaps he was exhausted, because he curled up in the gloomy basket and fell fast asleep, even though the wind whistled through the wickerwork and blew his fur the wrong way round.

CHAPTER NINE

MILDRED sat hunched on her broomstick, feeling tired and anxious. She was beginning to feel that the Operation Rescue Tabby plan had been a mistake. Even if no one noticed that firstly Tabby was missing from the kitchen and secondly Ebony had resumed residence, she wouldn't ever be able to let Tabby out at Gloom Castle or everyone would know. Perhaps she could just keep him in her room and only let him out at night when everyone was in bed, or if they had to share a room

she could choose Maud and then let her in on the secret.

"There it is, girls!" Miss Cackle called out so suddenly that everyone jumped.

"There's the coast, and there's Gloom Castle. What a spectacular sight!"

The coastline was indeed a spectacular sight, though not exactly what the pupils of Form Two had hoped for.

For a start, the sun had disappeared behind ink-black clouds and it was just beginning to rain. Then there was the coastline itself, which consisted of mile after mile of amazingly high and rugged cliffs meeting an angry-looking navy-blue sea amid a mass of jagged rocks and shadowy coves. The waves smashed against the cliffs, sending up clouds of spray so high

that the convoy of pupils and teachers could taste the salt in the air.

"Look, Mildred," said Maud, pointing to the castle, which was the only habitation in sight as far as they could see.

Gloom Castle looked even more forbidding than Miss Cackle's Academy. Delicate scarves of mist and sea spray hung around its battlements. The windows were slit windows, like those at the Academy, but larger, so that more wind could howl up and down the corridors, and seagulls perched screeching on every rooftop and window ledge.

What seemed like several miles below was Grim Cove, with a tiny shingle-and-stone beach, a rather sinister-looking cave, a small boat at anchor, and a large rock shaped like a cat's head about half a mile out to sea. There were hundreds of tiny steps cut into the cliff face leading down from the castle to the bay.

Mildred shuddered. "No wonder they call it Grim Cove!" she muttered, as a squall of rain hit them like a water cannon.

"Begin the descent, girls!" Miss Hardbroom's military voice whipped along the wind. "Head for the inner courtyard."

The descent was more difficult than normal, for various reasons. First of all it was difficult to see where they were going, with their cloaks tying themselves in knots and the blinding rain and wind in their faces, and secondly they did not know the layout of the castle and were attempting to land in a small enclosed courtyard inside the battlements.

To do this, they had to hover like helicopters and inch their way downward. Even Ethel found it heavy going, but eventually they all arrived in the rain-lashed courtyard, soaked to the skin and frozen stiff. Fortunately for Mildred nearly all the cats were yowling and screaming with rage, as the rain had driven in through their baskets and drenched them. No one gave Tabby a second thought.

The girls lined up in their usual rows trying to look as neat as possible under the circumstances, while Miss Hardbroom smoothed her hair and robes and Miss Cackle adjusted her hat.

Without any warning, the two carved wooden doors leading into the yard burst open, and there was Mr. Rowan-Webb standing at the top of the stone stairs smiling at them.

"Welcome! Welcome!" he said, waving a hand into the dark corridor behind him. "What a foul day to make such a journey. Come in at once and get yourselves warm.

He looked a lot better than when they had last seen him, which was at Hallowe'en, when Mildred had presented him to the Chief Magician, Mr. Hellibore, and he had been changed from a frog to a human again. Then, his clothes were in rags, but now they were magnificent— a fine shade of emerald green with a bottle-green cloak and pointed hat. The cloak was beautifully embroidered all over with rainbow-coloured stars and moons.

Miss Cackle and Miss Hardbroom led the way up the steps into the castle and Form Two followed meekly behind, leaving wet footprints where they trooped along. The doors swung silently closed behind them, shutting out almost all the light except for a dim lantern hanging on the wall every few yards or so.

They made a curious sight, walking in single file with their broomsticks and bags

hovering along behind them, and the dis-
gruntled cats miaowing crossly from the
depths of the baskets. The dim lanterns
threw huge shadows up the walls as they
passed by.

Mr. Rowan-Webb led them into a huge stone hall very like the one at Miss Cackle's Academy only more sparsely furnished and much more draughty. There was a fireplace the size of an ice cream van, but sadly no fire.

"Do sit down, ladies," said Mr. Rowan-Webb, indicating several faded sofas and chairs, most of them with the springs and stuffing hanging out. "You must be worn out after all that flying."

Miss Hardbroom turned to the pupils,

who were standing in a soggy huddle, unsure whether "ladies" referred to them as well as Miss Hardbroom and their headmistress.

"You may sit down, girls," said Miss Hardbroom. "Tell your broomsticks to stand at ease."

"So sorry about the weather," apologized Mr. Rowan-Webb. "It's usually quite pleasant at this time of year. Anyway, there's a nice fire to warm you all up until I show you to your rooms."

Everyone looked pointedly at the empty grate.

Mr. Rowan-Webb looked too.

"Dear me!" he exclaimed. "Do forgive me, ladies. I really am so absentminded these days."

He muttered the words of a spell, waved his arms at the fireplace, and with a *whoosh!* a glorious log fire appeared, banked several feet high and throwing out such a fierce heat that those nearest had to back away.

"Now then, where was I?" said Mr. Rowan-Webb. "Oh, yes—rooms. I've given you three rooms in the west wing. One small room each for you, Miss Cackle, and you, Miss Hardbroom, and a large

dormitory for all the girls. The girls' dormitory only has camp beds and cushions and sleeping bags—rather a ragbag of bedding, I'm afraid. There are only two proper guest rooms with brass bedsteads, and naturally those are for the teachers. Never mind; it's all fun on holiday, isn't it?"

"I shan't be here during the week, though I shall come back on the last day. I'm still visiting various friends and relations whom I haven't seen for decades, since my awful incarceration in the Academy pond, and I promised Aunt Ethelburga a few days of my time.

"Now then, what else do I have to tell you—oh, yes, there is a boat in the cove, but I think it's best not to take her out, as there are rather a lot of rocks round and about. Any questions before you set off to unpack your things?"

No one dared to speak.

"Come along now, girls," said Miss Cackle cheerily. "Don't be shy. There must be something you'd like to know."

Enid put up her hand.

"I was wondering, Mr. Rowan-Webb," she said, "if there are any legends or stories about caves or smugglers around the castle and cove."

214

"There's only one tale *I've* ever heard," said Mr. Rowan-Webb. "There's a strange rock shaped like a cat's head, out to sea directly in front of the cove. A local tale tells how a sailor was once shipwrecked and

struggled to the rock in raging seas, holding on to a chest full of gold and silver coins and jewellery. He crammed the chest into a crevice in the rock and swam to the shore when the sea had calmed. But when he went back by boat with friends to collect the chest, he couldn't find it. Legend says that it is still there somewhere on Cat's Head Rock. I must say it would be rather handy to find it, as the rock belongs to me and I could do with the money for a few repairs to the castle! It's so difficult to get to it by boat, what with the currents and rocks, that no one has ever really bothered to investigate, especially as it probably isn't a true story anyway. Any other questions?"

No one else spoke.

"Right," said Mr. Rowan-Webb. "If you've all warmed up a bit, allow me to show you to your rooms."

CHAPTER TEN

THE DORMITORY was even more depressing than the castle and the coastline. Form Two stood and looked around in horror after they had been left to unpack.

There was a row of glassless windows at either end, which made the room like a wind tunnel. Enough beds for all the pupils lined the other two walls, but they were, as the magician had said, a rather poor assembly of camp beds, heaps of cushions, moth-eaten foam rubber and ancient, cardboard-stiff blankets. The beds nearest to the windows were wet from the rain, which sprayed and dripped its way in.

Ethel dived for the only proper bed with a mattress, in the centre of one of the rows, and plonked her bags and broomstick on top.

"Bags I this one!" she announced. "What a dump! Thanks for the holiday, Mildred Hubble. It's going to be a laugh a minute. At least the Academy will seem like a *real* holiday camp after a week in this place."

Mildred didn't reply, as the entire form was now scrambling for the best selection of beds.

"Come on, Mil!" called Enid, diving onto what looked like an old hospital trolley. "There's a camp bed next to mine with two blankets on!"

"No, there isn't!" exclaimed Drusilla, a friend of Ethel, who barged Mildred out of the way and slammed her belongings on to the camp bed with such force that it collapsed to the floor.

Mildred saw that the only place left was the worst one of all—a woven rush mat with a mildew-coloured sleeping bag, laid directly underneath the window.

"Thanks for trying, Enid," said Mildred, arranging her suitcase and broom against the wall and sitting down on the mat with the cat basket hugged to her chest.

All the other members of Form Two were busily letting out their cats for a stroll and a stretch, and the room was suddenly full of black cats miaowing and entwining themselves round their owners' legs.

"Aren't you going to give Ebony some exercise?" asked Maud from her position four beds away, as she cuddled her own cat, Midnight.

Mildred shot to her feet.

"Er, I think I'm going to take him to Miss Hardbroom," she said. "Just in case he really *is* ill after making all that noise on the way here."

And before anyone else could comment on the matter, she seized the basket and rushed out of the room.

Outside in the dark corridor, she stopped to contemplate what she was going to do with Tabby, now that they were all stuck in the same dormitory. If Ethel or Drusilla or anyone except Maud and Enid found out that she had defied the headmistress to bring Tabby, she would be in serious trouble.

As she stood and looked out of the window at the cove far below, she saw the boat bobbing up and down attached to a small breakwater, and a plan dawned in her mind like the thin shaft of sunlight which pierced the inky clouds above the castle.

"Come on, Tab," she whispered. "You're not going to like this one tiny bit, but it's the only solution."

CHAPTER ELEVEN

MAUD CARRIED her cat across to Enid's trolley and sat down next to her friend. Enid looked up from sorting out piles of grey socks and underwear.

"Mildred's *up* to something," said Maud darkly. "I just know it."

"Well, I wish she'd let *us* in on the secret," said Enid crossly. "She's been really strange for weeks—sort of vague and not quite with it."

A shriek of laughter rang out from Ethel, who had overheard.

"*Do* forgive me for stating the obvious, Maud," she said, "but Mildred Hubble is *permanently* vague and not quite with it. If *I* were you, *I'd* start worrying if she was

suddenly alert and getting A-plus for everything!"

"Oh, do stop it, Ethel," said Maud. "No wonder Mildred gets in such a state with the likes of you hurling insults at her all the time. Anyway, you shouldn't be

eavesdropping on other people's conversations. It's not right. Come on, Enid, let's move up to the other end so no one can hear us."

If they had glanced out of the window at that moment, they would have seen Mildred, plus her cat basket, making her way with great care down the cliff face to the cove.

The rain had eased off to an unpleasant misty drizzle, which covered Mildred's clothes and hair in a fine net of droplets.

The wind had suddenly abated, which made the descent far less terrifying than Mildred had expected, though the wooden handrail had rotted away in places and the steps were very slippery from the rain and sea spray.

Although she was most relieved to arrive all in one piece on the pebbly beach below, the sight of the sinister breakers relentlessly pounding into sizzling foam as they clawed at the shingle made Mildred's heart begin to pound like the waves themselves.

Beyond the cove, which was actually quite sheltered from the wind by the height and shape of the cliff, the sea swelled alarmingly, as if a gigantic monster was breathing just beneath the surface and the strange Cat's Head Rock sat bang in the middle of the horizon with white crests appearing where the waves dashed against it.

"What a truly awful place, Tabby," whispered Mildred into the wicker basket. "I should have left you in the nice warm kitchen instead of bringing you here. I'm so sorry, little cat. What a mistress you're lumbered with—and to think that Miss Cackle thought *I* was stuck with *you*."

First of all, Mildred examined the cave in the hope that it might be full of nice dry ledges and crannies, but it was unfortunately very shallow, more like a windblown sentry box, with not one projection in the rock to hide a cat basket. The boat was the only other hope.

Mildred opened the basket and let Tabby out for a run. Tabby looked most unimpressed by the sight of so much water, and stalked off to examine the cave, leaving Mildred to edge along the breakwater so that she could take a good look at the boat.

It was bigger than it had looked from Gloom Castle. There were two benches for rowers to sit on, and at one end was a little cabin with a tiny door and window. A pair of oars was neatly lashed to the inside of the boat and there was a life belt

on the side of the cabin, which made Mildred feel a little less panic-stricken.

Very carefully, Mildred lowered herself into the boat, which rolled alarmingly until she had found her balance, opened the door into the cabin, and squeezed herself inside.

It was surprisingly snug. The rhythmic movement of the waves and the muffled slapping of the water even felt quite soothing after all the howling wind and rain. It really did seem the perfect place to hide a striped cat who shouldn't have come on holiday in the first place.

CHAPTER TWELVE

WHERE'S Ebony, Mil?" asked Maud, as Mildred arrived back in the dormitory carrying the cat basket with the door open. "He's all right, isn't he?"

"I don't know," said Mildred. "He jumped out when I was on my way to Miss Hardbroom, and disappeared out of the nearest window along the battlements. I expect he'll be back soon. He's a more adventurous cat than Tabby."

At least *that* part's true! she thought miserably, feeling terrible at telling such an appalling number of lies to her best friend.

"*I* think Miss Cackle should have let you keep that moth-eaten stripy rug," jeered Ethel, whose clothes were now all folded into regimented piles on top of her suitcase at the end of her bed. "No wonder poor old Ebony's made a bolt for it!"

Mildred had been working very hard on her spells and could now remember word-perfect the spells to change people into pigs, snails, frogs, and centipedes, plus the antidote spells to change them back. She was sorely tempted to lash out and turn Ethel into a centipede for ten minutes, but managed to restrain herself when she remembered the other occasion, in her first term, when she had got into the most awful trouble with Miss Hardbroom for changing Ethel into a pig.

Just at that moment, as if to remind Mildred that it wouldn't have been a good idea at all, Miss Hardbroom materialized in the middle of the room.

"Excellent, Ethel," she said, a wave of her bony hand indicating Ethel's neat pile of belongings. "If only you all had such organized brains as Ethel Hallow, Form Two. Ethel could make a rubbish heap look like an army barracks—even her cat knows how to arrange itself with taste."

Ethel's cat, Night Star, was sitting bolt upright with his head slightly bowed on top of a pile of cardigans, looking like a statue from a museum.

"Yuk!" whispered Mildred to Maud. "Doesn't she make you feel sick?"

"I do hope you aren't referring to *me*, Mildred Hubble?" said Miss Hardbroom icily.

"Oh, no, Miss Hardbroom," said Mildred, blushing.

"Then who *were* you referring to, Mildred?" asked Miss Hardbroom.

"Ethel Hallow, Miss Hardbroom," muttered Mildred.

"Envy of Ethel's superior qualities will get you absolutely nowhere, Mildred Hubble," snapped Miss Hardbroom. "Apologize to Ethel, please."

"Sorry, Ethel," mumbled Mildred.

"That's all right, Mildred," Ethel said, smiling sweetly. "We all know you can't help it."

"Now then, girls," said Miss Hardbroom. "The rest of the day is yours to study and rest after the long flight. Then we will have an early bedtime and hope that the weather is a little less bracing tomorrow so that we can play some games and sports on the beach."

Having said this, she vanished.

Everyone stood around, looking nervous. No one dared to speak for several minutes, as they were never sure if she was still there or not.

Ethel was the first to speak, saying, just to be on the safe side, "Well, I'm going to sit on my bed and brush up on my chanting. We've got a test during the week, holiday or not."

"Good girl, Ethel," Miss Hardbroom's approving tones wafted through the room, making everyone jump.

There was a hasty scramble as the pupils of Form Two all dived for their beds and took out their spell and chanting books and arranged themselves in as studious-looking positions as possible.

After a while, everyone relaxed and began chatting again.

"What will you do if Ebony doesn't come back?" Enid called across the other beds to Mildred.

"Oh, he'll be back," said Mildred vaguely. "And even if he's gone for a few days, I'm sure he'll be back in time to go home."

CHAPTER THIRTEEN

WHEN MILDRED woke up the next morning, she had a stiff neck from sleeping beneath the window. She sat up to peer out through the mist and saw a watery sun lurking behind the clouds.

Her first thought was for Tabby, and she crept out of her sleeping bag and clambered into her sports kit of grey aertex shirt, knee-length black shorts, grey socks, and black plimsolls. (Miss Hardbroom and Miss Cackle had decreed that everyone was allowed to wear sports clothes for the entire holiday.) As it was still very early and rather cold, she wrapped her cloak around her shoulders and tiptoed out of the dormitory.

Seagulls screamed and wheeled around her as she picked her way carefully down the rickety steps to the cove. To Mildred's delight, the sun had burnt through the clouds and the mist rolled back across the sea, as if an invisible hand was rolling up

a carpet before her very eyes, and there below her lay the sea, sparkling and calm, the boat gently bobbing like a bath toy at the end of the breakwater.

Mildred's spirits lifted like the mist as the sun warmed her tousled morning hair, and she watched the sea turn bluer by the minute. It seemed a completely different place from yesterday.

Tabby was curled up on a pile of rope inside the shelter at the end of the boat. Mildred could see him as she peeped in through the window.

"Good morning, Tab!" she said, opening the door. "I've brought your breakfast."

Tabby sprang onto her shoulder with one bound and rubbed his head against her neck. He certainly seemed none the worse for his night on board the boat.

Mildred unwrapped the little parcel of food which she had brought. She had saved three fish fingers and a lump of soggy mashed potato from dinner the night before. In fact, it was nearly *all* the dinner, as they had only had five fish fingers to start with, as well as baked beans, but she knew Tabby didn't like baked beans, so she had gratefully eaten those herself. She had also brought some milk mixed with water, in a plastic bottle she had saved from their breakfast on the flight to the castle.

Mildred went and sat on the shingle beach and watched Tabby exploring the seaweed.

"I'd better get back, Tab," said Mildred after a while. "They'll all come to investigate if they know I'm down here so early. I'll leave the window open a bit, so you don't get too hot. At least there's a nice breeze on the sea. I'll come back this evening and let you out again. Don't you worry, now."

245

Tabby wasn't at all keen about going back into the cabin. Mildred had to rugby-tackle him and stuff him protesting back inside.

Everyone was up and in the middle of dressing when Mildred arrived back in the dormitory.

"Well, fancy that," said Ethel. "Mildred Hubble the early riser. Been practising your broomstick water-skiing have you?"

"Something like that," muttered Mildred.

"What a terrific morning!" exclaimed Maud, smiling joyfully as she looked out of the window. "Miss Hardbroom just came in and announced that we're to spend the whole day on the beach! We've all got our swimming costumes on under our PE clothes, Mil. You'd better get yours on too—oh, and don't forget to bring your swimming hat and your broomstick. The magician's arranged for us to have breakfast on the beach as a special treat!"

Not too near the boat, I hope! thought Mildred, anxious that someone might hear or see Tabby.

Miss Cackle and Miss Hardbroom were waiting for the members of Form Two in the little courtyard.

"Good morning, girls," said Miss Cackle, beaming. "Such glorious weather, after yesterday."

"I hope you're all very grateful to be here having this wonderful holiday," snarled Miss Hardbroom, making them all feel guilty as usual.

"Yes, Miss Hardbroom," chorused the girls.

"Yes, yes, Miss Hardbroom," said Miss Cackle. "I'm sure we're *all* delighted to be here. Now then, as we all have our broomsticks with us, we may as well fly down to the cove instead of using those rather worn-looking steps. Mr. Rowan-Webb has left a veritable feast of a breakfast on the beach, so the sooner we get down there the better, *I* say! Take it easy on the way down—the cliffs are very steep. I think we should hover our way down rather than attempting a nosedive."

CHAPTER FOURTEEN

BREAKFAST consisted of the most delicious array of food. The girls were dumbfounded at the amount of choice. In fact, there was usually no choice at all, just grey porridge looking like half-set concrete.

"Don't just stand there gawping, Form Two," said Miss Hardbroom. "Take a plate and anything you require. Anyone would think you'd never *seen* food before."

The feast was spread out on two long trestle tables. There were several jugs of orange juice, two silver dishes full of kippers (Mildred made a mental note that she must get one or two for Tabby), ten silver racks stuffed with toast, pots of butter, four huge jars of marmalade, two pots of Marmite, three silver dishes full of crispy bacon, a large dish of grilled tomatoes, and two more loaves in case anyone was still hungry.

There was also a large pottery urn full of cornflakes and two pottery jugs full of milk, plus several bowls of sugar. The bowls and plates were all a beautiful shade of midnight blue with tiny gold stars on them. The girls still didn't quite dare to help themselves.

"Tuck in, girls!" announced Miss Cackle. "*I'm* certainly not going to wait a moment longer!"

This was the signal they all needed, and soon there was a noisy bustle of spoons and bowls being grabbed and everyone was piling up as much food as they could cram on to their plates.

"Steady on, Mil!" said Maud, as she noticed Mildred attempting to hide three kippers underneath two strategically placed pieces of toast.

"I'm *starving* this morning," said Mildred. "It must be the sea air!"

She had a plastic bag in the pocket of her voluminous shorts, and managed to slide in all three kippers with the minimum of mess while no one was looking.

After the girls had eaten everything in sight and were lolling around feeling so full that they could hardly breathe, Miss Cackle clapped her hands and chanted the words of a spell no one had heard before. At once the trestle tables took off like a pair of giant seagulls and flew back up the cliff, where they disappeared out of sight into the castle.

"Mr. Rowan-Webb lent me that spell, girls," said Miss Cackle, "as part of our breakfast treat—no washing up for anyone this morning!"

Form Two cheered loudly.

"Now then, girls!" announced Miss Hardbroom. "First of all, a word of warning. When your broomsticks are near the water their magic powers are far less efficient. That is to say, they don't work so brilliantly when their magic is damp. Of course in *some* people's cases, they don't work too brilliantly even in ninety degrees of heat." Here she shot a glance at Mildred, who dropped her eyes to the beach, feeling aware of the illicit kippers congealing in her pocket. "For this reason," Miss Hardbroom went on, "you will find it difficult to keep your broomsticks stable directly above the water. However, if the broomsticks are hovering a good few feet above the waves, they will be strong enough to pull you along behind on water skis. Miss Cackle and I have stored the school skis in a crate in the cave, which you will see behind us. There are enough pairs to fit every girl, plus one piece of rope each.

Please go and collect these items and come back to me."

Thank goodness I didn't hide Tabby in the cave, thought Mildred, as she joined the scrum of pupils grabbing their equipment.

"This should be fun!" exclaimed Enid, emerging laden from the cave just as Mildred was going in.

"Has anyone tried broomstick water-skiing before?" asked Miss Hardbroom once the girls had lined up on the beach with all their gear.

"I don't mean to boast, Miss Hardbroom," simpered Ethel, "but I was champion at my junior school."

"Excellent, my dear!" enthused Miss Hardbroom. "Then perhaps you could show your fellow pupils what is required."

Ethel set about fixing the length of rope onto the back of the broomstick. There was enough spare to leave several feet of rope, which she tied into a handle at the other end.

"Shall I give a demonstration, Miss Hardbroom?" asked Ethel.

"Thank you, Ethel," said Miss Hardbroom. "That would be most kind."

Ethel took off her sports clothes to reveal her striped bathing costume. She bundled her hair into the black bathing hat and carried her broomstick and the skis to the shallow water at the edge of the beach.

"Hover!" she commanded her broom, which remained lifeless in her hands. "Miss Hardbroom—it won't hover!" Ethel was close to tears. "This has never happened before, Miss Hardbroom— Miss Cackle, I'm so sorry!"

"Don't worry, Ethel!" called Miss Hard-broom. "You've probably forgotten that it's a little too close to the water. Hold it above your head, dear."

Ethel laughed to hide her mistake. She held the broomstick as high above her head as possible while standing on tiptoe.

"Hover!" she commanded. This time the broomstick was perfectly happy to remain in midair. "Stay!" Ethel brandished a finger at the disobedient broom.

Then she sat in the water, pulled on her skis, and hunched up so that her shoulders were under the water. She held on to the handle at the end of the rope. "Off you go!" she called.

The broomstick shot off like a rocket.

Ethel rose out of the water, perfectly balanced on the skis, and roared away, skimming the water in a cloud of spray. She executed a figure of eight, almost touching

the water as she leaned into the curves,
then came back to the beach in a straight
line, sinking gracefully into the waves at
the edge of the shingle as she arrived.

"Stay!" she called to the broomstick,

which screeched to a halt at once and remained hovering patiently in midair, with the rope dangling into the sea.

"Was that all right, Miss Hardbroom?" asked Ethel earnestly.

"Superb, Ethel!" replied Miss Hardbroom. "Quite simply, superb. Now then, Form Two, let's see if you can all raise yourselves to Ethel's standard by the end of the week. Of course, I realize that it is *unlikely*, but you can at least *try*. I will be joining you for a spin later in the morning. Will you be joining us, Miss Cackle?"

Miss Cackle looked appalled.

"Er! Oh, no, I don't think so, Miss Hardbroom!" she answered, looking embarrassed. "I'll be going in for a quick dip though—if the weather stays pleasant!"

The girls exchanged delighted glances as they imagined Miss Cackle in a swimming costume.

"The sea level will probably go up several feet if Miss Cackle goes swimming!" giggled Mildred.

"What was that, Mildred?" asked Miss Hardbroom.

"Um—I was just discussing the er—the laws of *science!*" replied Mildred. "You know: when you put stones in a jar of water and the water level goes up. I was wondering if, you know—with all this seawater around, we could try a little experiment later on, to see if—"

"I'm glad to note that you are suddenly so fascinated with the laws of science, Mildred," said Miss Hardbroom. "I must set you a little test to occupy your inquiring mind in case you get bored on the holiday."

"Thank you, Miss Hardbroom," said Mildred.

Maud and Enid prodded their friend as they all suppressed a major fit of the giggles.

CHAPTER FIFTEEN

UCH TO Mildred's surprise, the rest of the day was extremely enjoyable. Even Miss Hardbroom seemed relaxed and almost friendly as the sun beat down on the sheltered beach and the waves danced on the shingle.

Much to Form Two's delight, Miss Cackle emerged from the cave, which she had been using as a private dressing room, wearing an extremely tight knee-length bathing costume made of black-

and-grey spotted material, which showed every bulge. She was also wearing a frilly black bathing hat made of drooping rubber petals, like a giant chrysanthemum.

"Super day for a dip, girls!" she called as she picked her way painfully through the pebbles and plunged into the sea, sending up a cloud of spray like a big dipper crashing through the water trough.

"This is the life, eh, Mil?" said Maud as she floated past Mildred, who was hopping along on one foot, making swimming motions with her hands in the hope that no one would notice her deficiency in the swimming department. "Even Miss Hardbroom's having a sneaky sunbathe — look."

Mildred screwed up her eyes against the glare. Sure enough, Miss Hardbroom, though still demurely clad in a calf-length black dress, was sitting leaning against a rock with her legs stretched out in the sun and no shoes or stockings!

"Cor, look at that!" said Enid. "No stockings! Whatever next!"

Miss Hardbroom stood up at that point and looked out to where the three girls were standing. They all jumped and turned away.

"Come on!" said Maud. "Start swimming again. She probably heard every word."

"She certainly did, Maud Spellbody," hissed Miss Hardbroom's voice from behind them. "So you'd better be careful what you say."

The three friends spun round and there was Miss Hardbroom doing an elegant crawl behind them. She was now wearing a close-fitting mauve bathing hat and a black knee- and elbow-length swimsuit with a purple V set into the front. The whole transformation had taken place within the space of half a minute.

After Miss Hardbroom had joined them, no one felt inclined to splash about or have any more fun, and everyone was soon grimly swimming up and down in silent rows before sedately getting out and sitting on the beach, wrapped in their towels.

As the evening approached, Mildred didn't have a chance to sneak the kippers across to Tabby, with the boat in full view of everyone. In fact, it was rather embarrassing, as the kippers were beginning to smell awful after a day of being crammed into Mildred's shorts.

Mildred tried to hang back as everyone settled onto their broomsticks and began flying back to the castle in ones and twos. Unfortunately, Enid and Maud waited loyally as their friend took ages rolling up her swimming costume in a towel, then purposely dropping it and rolling it up again and retying her plimsolls three times in a desperate attempt to be the last one left on the beach.

"Come on, Mil!" said Maud. "We're having dinner as soon as we get back. Everything'll have gone by the time you get your laces perfect."

There was nothing for it but to go back to the castle, kippers and all, and return later when no one was looking. At least she could sneak some more food and perhaps some milk for Tabby.

CHAPTER SIXTEEN

AN OPPORTUNITY presented itself at dusk, as Form Two were having an hour of leisure before going to bed. Maud was darning a hole in the toe of a sock and Enid was reading a manual on broomstick water-skiing, while the rest of the girls were bustling about, similarly employed. No one seemed to notice as Mildred slunk out of the door and made her way to the cliff steps.

She was halfway down when, to her horror, a voice called out from behind, making her jump out of her skin. It was Ethel.

"Hey, Mildred," she called. "Mind if I join you?"

"Er—no," said Mildred. "Of course not.

"Where are you off to, then?" asked Ethel with an unpleasant smile. "It's a bit

dangerous on these steps, so I thought you might need some assistance with whatever it is. You know how clumsy you are!"

Ethel managed to say all this in a light, sincere tone of voice. If you hadn't known her, you would have thought she was genuinely concerned, instead of nosily trying to find out something secret.

"I was just going for a stroll on the beach," Mildred improvised. "I've got a bit of a headache, that's all."

"Then why didn't you go to Miss Hardbroom?" asked Ethel. "She'd have given you an aspirin or something. No, I think you're *up* to something, Mildred Hubble, and I'm going to get Miss Hardbroom and tell her, before it's too late and you get us *all* into trouble."

They had reached the bottom of the steps by this time.

"Look, Ethel," said Mildred. "If I tell you, will you *promise* not to let on? Even Maud and Enid don't know."

Ethel considered the matter. She felt quite pleased at being let in on a secret which even Mildred's best friends didn't know about.

"All right," she said. "I promise."

"OK . . ." said Mildred, racking her brains for a good story. "You remember the story about the treasure out on Cat's Head Rock? Well, I was going to go out there, on the boat, and have a little look around to see if I could find it. It's a nice calm evening and it seemed a good idea. I thought the magician would be really pleased to have the treasure to buy things for the castle. I wasn't going to go *now*, maybe a bit later when everyone's asleep. I was just going to have a look to see if the boat's seaworthy."

Ethel stared at Mildred.

"Well, *I* think it's a dreadful idea," she said. "The magician *told* us not to use the boat, and you'd probably wreck it or something—anyway, there probably isn't any treasure at all. I say, Mildred, you do smell *awful*. Don't you think it would be more to the point if you went back to the castle and had a bath? You smell like a crate of rotting fish."

"Actually," said Mildred, "I sat on a kipper this morning and haven't had time to wash my clothes. Perhaps you're right about the plan to get the treasure. I think I'll go back to the dorm and forget all about it."

They set off on the long climb back up the steps, Ethel leading the way. While Ethel's back was turned, Mildred took the kippers from her pocket and lobbed them onto the deck of the boat, meaning to

come back after dark and give them to
Tabby in the shelter. The window was just
too narrow for him to squeeze out, though
Mildred had seen him looking out during
the day. Amazingly, no one else had noticed, and any mewing had been drowned
by the sound of the waves and seagulls
and the shouts of the girls.

Miss Hardbroom looked out of her window at the perfect evening sky and decided to take a broomstick ride. She rarely
felt quite so pleased with life as she did to-
day. For some reason, the warm weather
and the delights of seabathing had made

her feel completely relaxed. Even the girls did not irritate her quite as much as usual—except for Mildred Hubble of course. Mildred would have irritated Miss Hardbroom whatever the weather was like. There was something about the girl that just *got* to Miss Hardbroom, like a scratchy label sewn into the neck of a dress. It even annoyed Miss Hardbroom that they were only invited on the holiday in the first place because of Mildred's action in saving Mr. Rowan-Webb from the pond. However, putting all irritation aside, Miss Hardbroom swirled her cape around her shoulders, commanded her broom to hover outside the window and the cat—which was a particularly beautiful, smooth, black one with olive-green eyes named Morgana—to sit on the end, and lowered herself onto it gracefully.

"Away!" she commanded. "To the cave."

Mildred and Ethel had just reached the top of the steps and they both ducked as Miss Hardbroom zoomed over their heads, rather like one of those low-flying fighter planes that sometimes appear from nowhere when you're out walking in the country. Miss Hardbroom did not see the two girls as she nose-dived down the cliff face and pulled up to a perfect landing next to the breakwater where the boat was tied.

A chilly breeze was coming from the sea and Miss Hardbroom wrapped her cloak around her as she put the broomstick into the cave to keep it from getting wet.

At once, Morgana sprang purposefully onto the breakwater and ran along to the boat. She had smelt the kippers and couldn't wait to investigate. Miss Hardbroom was intrigued to see the cat disappear into the boat. She was even more intrigued when she heard a desperate yowling and saw the scruffy-looking Tabby madly trying to squeeze himself out of the few inches of open window in the shelter. Poor Tabby was frantic with hunger, and the sight of Morgana eating his evening meal was too much to bear.

Miss Hardbroom climbed aboard the boat to investigate. She recognized Tabby immediately, and her eyebrows knitted together like storm clouds as she made her way through the boat to the shelter. A slight breeze had come up, and the boat was bobbing and swaying, making it difficult to keep her balance. Miss Hardbroom had forgotten her own cat, now crouched underneath one of the benches wolfing down the kippers as fast as possible.

The boat lurched and Miss Hardbroom unfortunately braced her foot on an unexpected piece of fish skin, which zipped her over backwards, banging her head on the seat as she fell. A shower of stars and exploding lights cascaded past her eyes as she lost consciousness. Then there was no sound, except for Tabby's pitiful mewing, Morgana's munching, and the sea slapping at the sides of the boat.

CHAPTER SEVENTEEN

OF COURSE, Ethel hadn't believed Mildred when she said that she had given up her plan to visit the rock. She felt quite sure that Mildred would go back again, perhaps after dark. Mildred was such a bad liar and schemer that she always gave herself away. Ethel could tell by the way Mildred kept glancing out of the window and wandering up and down the dormitory. Even Maud and Enid had noticed something was wrong.

"What's the matter, Mil?" asked Maud. "You look so jumpy all the time."

"Nothing!" exclaimed Mildred in a falsely bright voice. "Nothing at all!"

Ethel smiled secretly to herself. She had been a little worried in case Mildred actually did manage to take the boat to Cat's Head Rock and find the treasure. The thought of everyone praising Mildred's cleverness was just too upsetting for words. Of course, it was more likely that Mildred would sink the boat than find the treasure, but she might just do it.

Well, thought Ethel, there's one surefire way to make sure she doesn't get the chance.

Mildred decided to abandon Tabby's dinner for the night. She couldn't face another trip down the cliff, either by broomstick or on foot, so the best thing to do seemed to be to go to sleep and sneak out at the crack of dawn. She had completely forgotten the story she had made up to Ethel about the boat trip to Cat's Head Rock. In fact, she had completely forgotten Ethel until she saw her come back into the dormitory with an "I-know-something-you-don't-know" look all over her face.

Ethel had obviously been out again. Her hair was windswept and she was wearing her cloak, which she folded neatly on top of her suitcase before she came and stood at the foot of Mildred's mat.

"I wouldn't bother going on any trip if I were you," she announced.

"What trip?" asked Mildred, confused for a moment. "Oh, yes! The trip to the rock. Yes—well, as I told you, I decided against it. *You* know best about these things, Ethel."

"Just in case you change your mind," said Ethel darkly, "why don't you take a look out of the window?"

Mildred sprang to her feet and peered out into the darkening night. Far below, in

the deep shadow of the cove, she could just make out the shape of the boat, no longer attached to the breakwater, making its way steadily out into the open sea.

"Ethel you—you—" Words failed Mildred as she ran to the door, pulling on her cardigan and cloak over her pyjamas. "Why can't you ever leave anything alone?"

"Don't make such a fuss, Mildred!" said Ethel, feeling a little embarrassed, as half the class was now propped up in their beds, listening. "It's only a boat, for goodness' sake."

Only a boat! thought Mildred, as she raced through the stone corridors and began the descent down the rickety steps. It says a lot for her desperation to rescue Tabby that she didn't stop to remember that she was afraid of the dark.

CHAPTER EIGHTEEN

STANDING at the edge of the waves with her eyes as wide open as possible, Mildred tried to gauge how far the boat had progressed. It certainly seemed a long way away, and the growing breeze was a little alarming, ruffling white crests onto the edge of the waves. Fortunately, a perfect full moon was rising above the horizon, casting a strong enough light to make Mildred less desperate about being out alone in the dark. There seemed to be nothing she could do. She couldn't swim at all, not even the doggie paddle. If only she had a broomstick.

Suddenly, there was a loud miaow from the cave. Mildred's heart leapt—first in fright, then for joy as she thought that Tabby must have somehow got off the boat and be sheltering in the cave.

"Tabby!" she called as she ran to peer into the darkness, but the cat which pattered out to rub itself against her ankles was not a tabby, but a beautiful, sleek, black one. Mildred noticed the broomstick leaning against the wall just inside the cave as she bent down and picked up the cat.

"Now who do *you* belong to?" asked Mildred. "Hello? Is there anyone there?" she called into the dark corners of the cave.

The complete stillness of the cave was her reply. The cat was now entwining itself round the broomstick, which Mildred caught as it toppled over sideways.

"*I* know!" she exclaimed, as an idea struck her. "Here's your rescuer, Tabby! It won't take a minute on this to zoom out to the boat and bring you back! Perhaps I could even bring back the boat and no one would be any the wiser.

She did wonder who the broomstick and cat belonged to, but of course there was no reason to suppose that they were Miss Hardbroom's. Poor Mildred would have been even more terrified if she had known that she was setting out on Miss Hardbroom's best broomstick and that Miss Hardbroom herself was in the boat.

"Drat that Ethel!" she muttered as she

pulled her cape around her shoulders. "I know she didn't realize about Tabby, but it's still an awful thing to do to unmoor a boat and just shove it out to sea—and I just *know* I'm bound to get the blame if it isn't back at the breakwater by the morning. You stay here in this nice warm cave, little cat—I won't be long."

She pushed the cat firmly back into the cave as, to Mildred's surprise, it tried to jump onto the back of the broomstick, which was hovering patiently in midair as she had commanded it.

"Off we go, then!" said Mildred, climbing on and giving the stick a brisk tap, and they set off up the beach, skimming the waves like a hovercraft.

Unfortunately Mildred had forgotten Miss Hardbroom's warning about the broomstick not working if it was damp, and instead of rising above the water she ploughed straight into it.

There was enough air trapped under Mildred's cloak to hold her up amid the waves, giving her time to remember how Ethel had come to grief during the broomstick water-skiing because she didn't hold it high above the water. It was very hard

not to panic, but Mildred managed to tread water well enough to stop herself sinking. She grabbed the broomstick and held it as far up in the air as she could.

"Fly! *Please* fly!" she gasped. "Off we go, *nice* broom, *beautiful* broom. *Please*."

Perhaps it was the flattery that did it, despite the broomstick being completely waterlogged. Very jerkily it rose above

the waves, pulling Mildred out of the sea, water cascading from her clothes.

"Stop!" Mildred shouted rather suddenly as she realized that they were now ten feet in the air and rising. It had been difficult

to tell how far they had risen because the moon had disappeared completely behind a sinister-looking black cloud, and the night was suddenly very dark.

Mildred could hardly believe that she had got into quite such a dreadful situation. Hanging by both arms from a broomstick is extremely difficult, even when your clothes are not twice as heavy with water. Mildred realized that there was only a limited amount of time that she could hold on, so she had only one hope, and that was to find the boat and literally drop into it.

From her vantage point in midair, she frantically peered all around into the pitch dark and tried to see where it was.

To her great surprise, the broomstick suddenly gave a little twitch and set off in a most determined manner, as if it really knew where it was going. In fact, it *did* know where it was going. Magic broomsticks are very curious things. If they are owned by one person for a very long time (and Miss Hardbroom had kept this particular one for twenty-five years), they develop a strange kind of intuition about their owners. In the same way that a dog will stand at the front door and wag its tail when its master is getting off a bus at the end of the street, a broomstick can sometimes sense that its owner is nearby, and if the owner is in trouble, the sense is even more acute.

The broomstick flew on grimly until it stopped, just as suddenly, and hovered. Mildred felt desperate.

"Go on, broom!" she said. "You were doing really well."

But the broomstick didn't budge. Mildred's arms and fingers were almost numb with cold and pain from hanging on. She began to cry as she imagined the horror of being alone, unable to swim on the darkest of dark nights. It really was all her worst fears come true. Slowly her fingers loosened their grip; she let go completely and fell through the black night air towards the waiting sea.

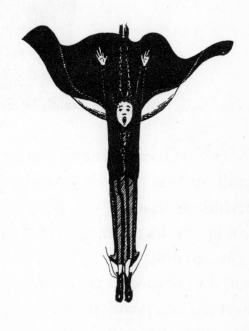

CHAPTER NINETEEN

INSTEAD of plunging into the soft, cold waves that she was expecting, Mildred landed with a jarring thud, half on something very hard, and half on something firm, but soft. She felt around and realized, partly from the rocking motion and partly from the feel of the planks, that it was a boat. She couldn't believe her luck when a loud miaowing began a few yards to her left.

"It's Tabby!" she gasped, feeling completely hysterical with relief. Fortunately, she remembered the broomstick. Although now it had found its owner, it would have hovered patiently above the boat till someone came to the rescue.

"Down, broom!" called Mildred. "Down here and rest!"

As it landed neatly next to her, Mildred flung her arms around it and gave it a hug.

"You brilliant, wonderful, *magic* broom!" she said. "Thanks a million, billion, trillion!" But the broomstick just stayed stiffly in her arms, like any old broom you might have found in a backyard somewhere, and when she let it go, it clattered to the deck, waiting for its next command. They're curious things, broomsticks.

Mildred got up to feel her way to the cabin and tripped over the soft thing she had half landed on. She put out her arms to try to ascertain what it was, and was

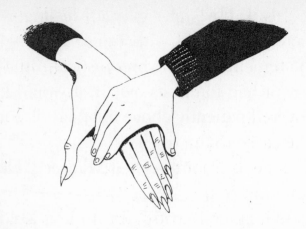

appalled when her fingers closed around a cold, bony hand. Mildred leapt back in horror, wondering if perhaps she was having some awful nightmare that might go away if only she could wake up.

With marvellous timing, the moon re-appeared from the scudding clouds for a brief moment and revealed various things to the petrified young witch. The first was the astonishing sight of Miss Hardbroom, apparently fast asleep on the floor of the boat. The second was dear old Tabby, still trying to scrabble his way out of the impossibly small opening in the window, and the third was the terrifying sight of Cat's Head Rock, looming like a gigantic sea monster only a few feet away.

The moon hung like a spotlight, as if some helpful person had decided to give Mildred a few clues, then, just as suddenly, the clouds closed over and it was dark again, though not as utterly dark as before. The clouds were not quite so dense this time and Mildred could still see the rock, as well as Miss Hardbroom stretched out at her feet.

Mildred groped her way to the prow of the boat and hauled in the long rope that had been untied and left trailing in the sea. There was only one thing to do. In the few seconds that the moon had flood-lit the scene, Mildred had noticed that the rock was full of jagged promontories and crevices. If she could somehow wedge the boat into a crevice and tie it to a projecting piece of rock, they could stay there until daylight. Perhaps by then Miss Hardbroom might be awake and full of bright ideas.

However, right now the wind was getting stronger by the minute and the waves higher, so Mildred had to think fast. In fact, it was amazing how sensibly she behaved on this occasion, bearing in mind how ghastly everything seemed and how scatterbrained she was most of the time.

"Come on, broom," she said. "The rescue isn't over yet."

She tied the rope as securely as possible onto the back of the broomstick, then held the broomstick up as high as possible.

"Off you go, broom!" she commanded. "Straight above the rock! Now! Fast as you can!"

The broom shot away like a missile,

towing the boat along behind it with surprising ease.

"Stop now!" called Mildred desperately,
a little too late, as the boat slammed into
the rock, wedging itself perfectly into a

boat-shaped crevice. She was thrown several feet down the boat, headfirst into the cabin door, where she very nearly joined Miss Hardbroom unconscious on the floor.

Mildred staggered to her feet and hauled the broomstick back into the boat. She untied the rope and retied it several times around a large barnacled piece of

rock, just in case the boat relaunched itself. In fact, it was quite a sheltered crevice, the wind being in the opposite direction and blowing the waves away from them.

Mildred opened the cabin door so that she could perhaps drag Miss Hardbroom inside, out of the cold, but the formidable

form mistress was too heavy to move, so
Mildred took off her sodden cloak, wrung it
out, and draped it over Miss Hardbroom to
keep out the wind. She sat hunched up next
to her teacher, rubbing the long, bony hands
in a useless attempt to warm them up.

Tabby escaped at last through the open
door and wrapped himself around

Mildred's shoulders. Mildred found him wonderfully warm and dry in the middle of all the wet clothes and breaking waves. She suddenly realized that Tabby could help to keep Miss Hardbroom warm, so she draped him around Miss Hardbroom's neck and told him to stay there.

She was so tired that she couldn't think anymore, so she leaned half against the

cabin and half against Miss Hardbroom
to help with keeping her warm, and closed
her eyes, hoping that perhaps it really *was* a
nightmare and any minute now the rising-
bell would clang through the dormitory
and wake her up.

CHAPTER TWENTY

ILDRED awoke to the sound of her name being shouted very loudly by several voices. For a moment she thought she was on her mat at the castle, where she had woken up so stiff and aching from the draught at the window. However, this stiffness was a hundred times worse, and her eyes felt puffy as she prised them open and looked around at the extraordinary sight. Miss Hardbroom was still in exactly the same position on the floor of the boat,

Tabby was asleep, purring, on Mildred's lap, the broomstick was lying across the two bench seats, and all around was a cloudless blue sky and a perfectly calm, innocent-looking sea. Mildred's clothes were so thoroughly wet that she couldn't imagine ever feeling warm again.

"Mildred! Mildred Hubble!" called a voice from the other side of the rock.

"Over here!" croaked Mildred. "I'm on the other side; over here!"

To Mildred's eternal delight, Maud and Enid zoomed into sight on their broomsticks and landed on the rock just above the boat. They couldn't believe their eyes when they saw Miss Hardbroom.

"Gosh, Mil!" said Maud. "I know you and Miss Hardbroom don't quite see eye to eye about things, but what on earth's happened?"

"*I* don't know," said Mildred. "I came to rescue Tabby, that's all, and Miss Hardbroom was in the boat when I found it. She's still breathing, but she's been unconscious for ages. We must get her back."

"What's Tabby doing here?" asked Enid. "He's supposed to be at the Academy!"

"Oh, I'll explain all that later," said Mildred. "I can't tell you how pleased I am to see you. It was really grim last night. I didn't think I'd make it."

"Everyone's out looking for you," explained Maud. "Poor Miss Cackle's nearly gone out of her mind with worry, although when she discovered that Miss Hardbroom was missing, she thought perhaps you might be all right together. Anyway, this morning we all broke up into groups and set off to find you."

"*I* know," said Mildred. "Let's tie the rope onto one of the broomsticks and let it fly us home. This one"—she patted Miss Hardbroom's recumbent broomstick— "was quite fantastic last night. I found it in the cave on the beach and it seemed to *know* where the boat was."

"That's because it's Miss Hardbroom's broomstick, silly!" said Maud. "Miss Cackle found her cat, Morgana, on the beach, so

317

she must have left her broomstick in the cave. . . . I say, Mil—Ethel must be having kittens. I mean, we all *heard* her say she'd let the boat out. Do you think she knew that Miss Hardbroom was in it?"

"Perhaps she knocked her out and pushed the boat out on purpose!" exclaimed Enid.

"Even Ethel's not *that* bad," said Mildred. "No, she pushed the boat out because I'd told her that I was taking it out to get the supposed treasure off this rock. I wasn't *really*. I was only going down the steps to feed Tab—I'd hidden him in the boat for the holiday. I made up the story to put Ethel off the scent. I suppose she couldn't bear the thought of me *possibly* finding the treasure. She didn't know about Tabby being on the boat and probably not about Miss Hardbroom either. She really *did* think it was just a boat. Anyway, let's get H.B. back to the castle as fast as possible. It can't be doing her any good lying here in those damp clothes. Ethel is an idiot— fancy doing all that just in case I upstaged her by finding some mythical treasure chest!"

Mildred began untying the rope from the projecting piece of rock and, as she did so, she noticed that the rock was a rather odd shape, not jagged or pointed, but with neat, sheared-off sides almost hidden beneath barnacles and fronds of seaweed. She scraped at the seaweed and a large, unmistakable hinge appeared. More scrap-

ing revealed a stout wooden plank and another and another.

"It's a chest!" gasped Mildred. "Look! It really is a chest!"

"We'll never get it free from the rock," said Enid. "It's practically grown into it—look."

"We could see if one of the broomsticks could pull it free," said Mildred. "Miss Hardbroom's broomstick seems to be as strong as an ox."

"Let's try!" said Maud.

So they untied the boat end of the rope and tied it firmly onto Miss Hardbroom's broomstick.

"Pull, broom!" said Mildred. "Pull as hard as you can and stop when I tell you."

The broomstick set off very fast, several feet above the water, until the rope was taut and the chest was wrenched with a sudden ripping of barnacles, years of sea and salt and swollen wood, clean out of the rockface, where it fell conveniently into the boat, narrowly missing Miss Hardbroom by a few inches.

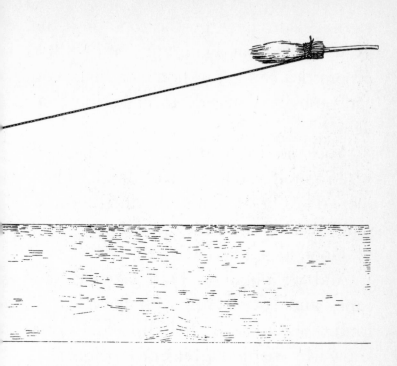

"Stop!" yelled Mildred. The broom was still pulling as firmly as possible, nearly turning the boat on its side. "Down and rest."

"Shall we try to open it?" asked Maud.

"It's very rusty," said Enid. "I think we'll need a crowbar."

"Or dynamite!" suggested Mildred. "No, first and foremost we *must* get H.B. back to the castle. Let's tie the rope onto the front of the boat again and see if H.B.'s broomstick can get us home. Perhaps you can both fly alongside to make the boat lighter."

"You and Tab can ride on the back of my broom if you like," said Maud. "Then there'd just be H.B. and the chest for it to pull."

"Good idea," said Mildred.

"And we ought to both take off our capes and cover H.B. with them," said Enid. "She must be half frozen. I don't know why we didn't think of it before."

Maud and Enid both took off their capes. Maud laid hers gently over their form mistress and Enid rolled hers up to make a pillow. Tabby, who had heard the conversation about taking him on Maud's broomstick, made a dive for the cabin and refused to come out.

"Never mind," said Mildred, scrambling onto the back of Maud's broom, which was hovering patiently with Maud already on it. "He doesn't weigh much; he might as well stay on board."

Miss Cackle was on the beach with various members of Form Two, who had come to report after making trips to search for Mildred and Miss Hardbroom.

"Look over there, girls!" exclaimed Miss Cackle. "Isn't that a boat in the distance with some of our girls flying above it?"

Everyone craned their necks and screwed up their eyes against the sun to get a clearer view, and as the boat came nearer they could see Mildred on the back of Maud's broom, Enid next to Maud, and the spare broomstick pulling the boat along. They all let out a rousing cheer of delight.

"Mildred Hubble!" called Miss Cackle, not sure whether to be thrilled or angry. "Come here at once and explain where on *earth* you have been, worrying us all senseless."

The boat coasted alongside the breakwater, expertly steered by the broomstick under Mildred's orders. Everyone ran to

help and stopped in their tracks when
they saw Miss Hardbroom lying in the
boat wrapped in the cloaks. Tabby chose
this moment to come miaowing out of the
cabin and jump onto the chest.

Miss Cackle stood and stared in complete bewilderment. So did all the other members of Form Two.

"Oh, dear," said Mildred. "This is all going to be very difficult to explain."

CHAPTER TWENTY-ONE

THE MAGICIAN arrived back early when he received word of Miss Hardbroom's accident. He materialized in a swirl of brilliant-coloured smoke in the middle of the courtyard, dusted himself down, and strode indoors, watched from the windows of their dormitory by the members of Form Two.

Mildred, Maud, and Enid climbed down from the window and sat in a row on Mildred's mat, each one cuddling her cat.

"At least I've got Tabby back for the day," said Mildred gloomily. "Though they're bound to be absolutely *raving* after last night. Goodness knows what'll happen."

Ethel looked very nervous too, which was most unusual for her.

"If any of you say *anything* about me pushing the boat out," said Ethel, "I'll—I'll—"

"Oh, it's all right, bossy boots," said Maud. "No one's going to sneak on you. *You're* the sneak around here, remember?"

Maud could be quite withering when she wanted to.

Suddenly, there was a knock on the door. They all leaped to their feet and stood by their assorted beds, thinking that it must be Miss Cackle, as Miss Hardbroom was in bed tucked up with a hot-water bottle, a bandaged head, and a pile of warm blankets.

But it wasn't Miss Cackle. It was the magician, and to everyone's surprise, he was smiling and looking just as genial as the day they had arrived.

"Mildred, my dear," he said. "Come with me." He led Mildred through the maze of passages to Miss Hardbroom's room where, to Mildred's relief mingled with terror, Miss Hardbroom was wide awake, sitting propped up in bed with a huge white bandage around her head. Miss Cackle was perched on a chair on the other side of the bed. Miss Cackle smiled in welcome, but Miss Hardbroom looked grim.

"Come in, Mildred," said Miss Cackle. "You'll be relieved to hear that Miss Hardbroom is perfectly all right after her terrible ordeal in the boat. I'm afraid she'll have to spend the rest of the holiday in bed after such a nasty knock on the head, but I'm sure you girls will be able to cope for a few days away from the firm guidance of your form mistress."

"Oh, yes, Miss Cackle!" agreed Mildred, sounding a little too eager.

Miss Hardbroom shot a menacing glance in her direction.

"I mean"—contrived Mildred hastily—"of course we'll soldier on and do our *best*, but it will all be much more difficult without Miss Hardbroom at the helm."

"All right, Mildred," muttered Miss Hardbroom. "There's no need to overdo it."

"Now then, Mildred," said Miss Cackle, rising from her chair and pushing her glasses on top of her head. "About yesterday's little escapade."

Oh, dear, thought Mildred. Here we go.

"If you hadn't disobeyed orders and brought that dreadful cat, which should have been in the kitchen catching mice," said Miss Cackle, looking serious, "Miss Hardbroom would not have climbed into the boat to investigate when she saw it at the window, thereby avoiding the fall which knocked her out."

"No, Miss Cackle," agreed Mildred, looking at the floor.

"However," continued Miss Cackle, "neither would you have discovered the chest which you brought back from the rock, which *is* after all the very same treasure chest described to you by the magician in the folktale about the shipwrecked sailor. Yes, Mildred, the chest is packed with gold coins and the most gorgeous jewellery."

Mildred didn't know how to react. She looked around the room, first at Miss Cackle, who was looking thrilled and excited, then at the magician, who was smiling at her with a vaguely fond expression, and finally at Miss Hardbroom, who looked as if she would like to expel her worst pupil on the spot.

"What will happen to Tabby?" she asked.

The magician stepped forward and put an arm around Mildred's shoulders.

"You must be so proud of this child, Miss Cackle," he said. "And especially you, Miss Hardbroom, after she saved your life. Most girls would want to know if they could have the

treasure, but not *this* girl. The only thing she wants in the world is her little cat, and I can't see any reason why she shouldn't have it, can you?"

"Well, I really don't think—" began Miss Hardbroom, but the magician cut across her.

"I mean to say, Miss Hardbroom, the cat actually wrapped itself around your neck to keep you warm all night. It's the least reward we can give to Mildred to let her keep her little lifesaver."

"If you think so, Your Honour," said Miss Hardbroom, trying to look gracious.

"And as for the treasure," said the magician, "there's enough to do all the repairs to the castle here *and* to give you a substantial amount for Miss Cackle's Academy."

"Oh, Mr. Rowan-Webb!" exclaimed Miss Cackle. "How simply wonderful. I've been wondering how we were going to

pay for the new roof on the west wing—
perhaps there'll even be enough left for a
swimming pool!"

"Could I go and tell Tabby the good
news?" asked Mildred, anxious to leave
the room before any more questions were
asked.

"Of course," said Miss Cackle.

"I'll escort you back to your dormitory,"
said the magician.

Just outside the dormitory door, the magician handed a small package to Mildred.

"This is a little present from the treasure chest," he said. "I thought you ought to have a memento, and it seemed rather appropriate. I still haven't forgotten how you rescued *me* last year. Enjoy the rest of your stay, my dear. It's bound to be a little easier with your form mistress recovering in her room."

The dormitory was empty, except for the cats. Everyone had been called to the hall for a late breakfast. Mildred could hardly wait to join them and share the wonderful news about Miss Hardbroom being out of action for the rest of the holiday. Before she left the room, she curled up for a quick hug of Tabby and to find out what was in the magician's package.

It was a gold chain with a delightful pendant composed of two golden frogs, one with emeralds for eyes, the other with rubies. They were sitting solemnly facing each other, shaking hands. Mildred put it

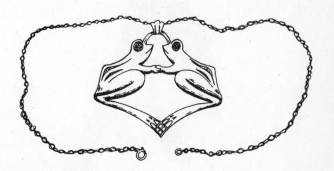

on and slipped it out of sight beneath her shirt as a secret good-luck charm, where she kept it for ever, even when she grew up. Certainly that day, as she raced down the sunlit stairs to find her friends and tell them all her news, she felt like the luckiest girl in the world instead of the worst witch in the school.

JILL MURPHY wrote *The Worst Witch,* the first book about the adventures of Mildred Hubble, at the age of eighteen. But she actually began writing and illustrating books as a small child, as soon as she could "hold a pencil." About her own school days, she says, "When I was in school, I used to imagine what it would be like if we were all allowed to bring our pets. I still think it would be nice to have a classroom full of pets." Jill Murphy is also well known for her very popular Mr. and Mrs. Large picture books, which detail the domestic chaos of an elephant family. *Five Minutes' Peace,* described by *The New York Times Book Review* as "painfully funny," was a *Parents* Best Book for Babies, and *All in One Piece* was highly commended for the Kate Greenaway Medal in England.